SADIE
THE SADIST

by

Zané Sachs

This book is a work of fiction. Any similarities to people, living or dead, are coincidental. If characters in this book remind you of anyone you know, please contact a psychiatrist or the police.

Cover by Jeroen ten Berge
Formatting by TERyvisions

for
all the good, hardworking people in supermarkets
and other service industries

Contents

Contents *(continued)*

CORN

I'M JUST *THINKING* ABOUT KILLING someone.

Most nights, when I get home from work, I lie in bed and stare into the darkness, my hands on fire. That's what comes from cutting, shucking, wrapping corn all day. My hands go numb, so does my brain.

But tonight my brain is working double time.

To do my job, you not only have to be a masochist, you need to be stoic: head down, no complaints, just keep cutting, shucking, wrapping. I do it for insurance and 'cause I need the money.

And maybe I'm a masochist.

Sometimes I call myself Sad Sadie, cry myself to sleep.

Not tonight. Tonight I'm sick of being sad. I'm ready to *think positive*, take charge and change my life.

I flip the switch. Light floods my bedroom, sends shockwaves through my brain.

My hands hurt when I flex my fingers. I imagine them encircling his neck, thumbs pressing into his larynx, his face the color of a beet.

The corporation has this slogan: *Our People Count.* All day long—as customers push carts along the aisles, comparing cans of beans, boxes of spaghetti, butchered animals, dead fish—the store pipes in music. Between songs they blast this message:

Enjoy shopping here?
Consider a career with us.
You'll loooove it!
Our people count.

Count what? Ears of corn?

(My career is chopping corn.)

They keep it cold in Produce. Since they started this remodel it's been close to freezing. The vegetables last longer in arctic conditions—keep those carrots happy. No big deal if people lose a few fingers to frostbite. It's so cold, the heat of summer feels like the dead of winter. I wear a heavy sweater and wool socks even in the dead of summer.

Is there a *dead* of summer or did I make that up?

It's the dead of summer now.

Chop, chop, chop.

Shuck, shuck, shuck.

Wrap, wrap, wrap.

No human should work like this hour after hour, day after day, for weeks on end. I told the store's Assistant Manager they need a robot.

He was not amused.

Said, "Keep chopping."

His name is Justus. Sounds like justice, but it's not. He's the kind of guy a lot of women go for: athletic, handsome, and a jerk. He struts around the supermarket looking for holes—empty spaces on the shelves. Then he comes down to Produce and tells me to chop more, shuck faster, get that corn upstairs. Once I mentioned processing so much corn is too much work for one person, suggested chopping, shucking, wrapping should be a group effort. If everyone in Produce chipped in, the job would be more efficient, go faster, could even be fun.

Not only did Justus ignore my suggestion, he added a third corn display—a *huge* endcap. (That's what they call those displays you see at the end of an aisle, enticing you to buy stuff you don't want.) Told me, "Keep it filled."

That's the kind of guy he is: Type A personality.

A for Ass.

That's why I can't sleep tonight.

His sorry ass is on my mind.

I push off the covers, get out of bed. Trying to distance myself from the throbbing pain, I pace my bedroom, stretch my fingers, shake my arms. This numbness hurts like hell— way beyond pins-and-needles, more like jolts of electricity short-circuiting my nerves. My hands look swollen and pasty, like rubber gloves filled with water.

We go through lots of rubber gloves down in Produce.

I say *down*, because vegetables and fruit are kept in the store's basement. The basement is also where you'll find the Produce cooler and the workroom where I chop and shuck. After checking on the corn displays upstairs—5-packs, 3-packs, 9s—I head down. Thanks to the remodel, we have a new freight elevator. It's scary cool.

Management posted a day-glow pink warning sign:

Attention!
Keep all hands and body parts inside the elevator
At all times
There's no sensor to stop the doors
Stand clear!

Body parts.

That's a giggle.

The elevator door slides open, revealing a metal mouth. A slab of steel moves up, as another slab descends—beyond the lips of steel: a metal grill. The grill's teeth lift and I step inside the mouth, careful not to touch triggers which (I've been warned) will set the jaws in motion. Once the jaws begin to close, there's no stopping them. Those slabs of steel could crush a skull, easy as a watermelon.

I press **B**, hear the beeping sound, and stand back from the door.

The elevator deposits me in the bowels of the building, next to Produce, across from the trash compactor. The compactor is big and smells like crap. Not surprising, since we toss a ton of rotting food into the pit. They tell you, don't climb into the compactor. Like anyone would step into that hole of filth. But I guess someone has, or why mention it?

When you open the compactor door, a blast of stink comes out: moldy vegetables, putrefying chicken, fish guts, the Assistant Manager's decomposing torso. (Wishful thinking.) To dump garbage, I lift the bag past my shoulders, above my head. I'm in good shape, but I'm only five foot two, and bench pressing trash bags filled with corncobs isn't easy. Bits of corncobs weigh a lot. The bags are too heavy for me to toss, so I use a broom to shove the trash all the way in. Then I press a button and the compactor crunches everything. The compressed trash is deposited into a giant dumpster. They keep the dumpster locked, so divers can't steal food. You wouldn't believe how much good stuff we throw away.

Once, I asked Justus if I could buy a roasted chicken for half price.

He looked at me like I'd suggested he rob a bank, and said, "That's against corporate policy, Sadie."

Then he tossed a dozen chickens into the compactor.

The basement is a twilight world, shadowy and creepy. To save energy, the lights are on a sensor, so unless something is moving, the hallways and the rooms are dark. No windows. I push through the heavy plastic doors leading into Produce, catch a whiff of cilantro, and wait for the sensor to detect me. The fluorescents flicker on, revealing crates of vegetables and fruit stacked to the ceiling, some on carts called U-boats, others on square pallets, so big and heavy that you need a pallet jack to move them. I can barely squeeze into my station. Any day now, I expect an avalanche of vegetables will smother me. The Produce guys process celery, lettuce, broccoli, that kind of stuff, at the sink up front. They pull off bad leaves, wash the produce in a salt solution, and wrap it with a band, so it looks nice.

I work at the triple sinks, in back, near the walk-in cooler. Actually, my workstation has four sinks. One for washing Salad Bar containers and utensils, a middle sink for rinsing, and a third sink for soaking in a chlorine solution. Across from the triple sink, there's a stainless steel counter and a deep utility sink with a garbage disposal—that's where I wash my fruit and vegetables. A line of knives hangs on the wall: three machetes for cutting things like watermelon (or heads), two chef's knives, and a selection of paring knives.

Did you know a sharp knife is safer than a dull one?

A sharp knife leaves a cleaner cut.

My job title is **Salad Bar**. Before corn season hit, my days were varied. First thing, I'd check the Salad Bar and process the vegetables we needed, then I'd work on fruit. I especially enjoyed cutting and arranging fruit, because it made use of my artistic talents—carving melons, selecting berries, peeling kiwis—paying close attention to color and texture as I arranged fruit in containers. Then I'd make specialty items like stuffed mushrooms and veggie kabobs, assembling them so they look appealing. I consider myself an artist of found objects. Right now I work with fruit and vegetables, but I plan to experiment with different mediums.

The point is, before corn season, my hands never went numb.

Before corn season, I enjoyed my job.

Cut fruit was my priority. I'd design it, bring it upstairs, and display my creations in the cut fruit case at the entrance of the store. I took pride in my work and enjoyed interacting with customers. I'd give out samples, make suggestions, help people find things—spent lots of time doing that.

Thanks to the remodel, finding things around the store has become a treasure hunt. For example, bandages have been moved from Aisle 13 to Aisle 5 next to macaroni, and you'll find mushrooms on the same aisle as cookie mix. Don't ask me why garlic and shallots are now on the tomato table instead of with the onions. Justus says the corporation spends a lot of money figuring out where to put things so no one can find them.

Before I was banished to the basement, I enjoyed being upstairs helping people.

Now I spend most of my time alone.

Reminds me of my childhood.

Sometimes my dad locked me in the basement.

These days, I arrive in the afternoon when the store is crazy busy, go right downstairs, find a pallet of corn (hidden behind a mountain of grapes), and start chopping. I use this cutter. It's real sharp. I call it my guillotine. Wait a second.

My fingers are killing me.

Usually, thinking about something else helps me forget the pain, but not tonight. I shake my hands, trying to wake them, walk around in circles. It feels like some kind of medieval torture. Like I'm stretched out on the rack, or hanging by my wrists. Pain pulses from my neck down through my arms, intensely hot, my nerves on fire. My fingers sting, like they're being jabbed with thousands of electric wires. Hurts so bad, I want to chop them off.

My guillotine would do the job.

Like I was telling you, that blade is sharp enough to slice through bone. When you're not using it, you have to keep it locked.

I place each piece of corn beneath the blade, to ensure the cut is clean and straight, chop off the shank—slicing through the soft chaff, the woody ring, the inner pith—then I flip the ear and chop off the tassel. Throw the ear into an empty box. For each crate, I repeat this process forty-eight times. If the corn is good, I get nine 5-packs and one 3-pack, but sometimes it's so rotten and full of worms that I have to toss half of it. I've gotten fast at chopping; cutting a crate takes about five minutes. It's the shucking that consumes my time: peeling down the husk, twisting off the silk, placing each ear carefully into a crate so the kernels aren't damaged. All that twisting does a number on your wrists. After the ears are shucked, I stack them in pyramids of three or five or nine, wrap them in plastic, stick on labels. The whole process, cutting, shucking, wrapping, takes about thirty minutes per crate—no stopping, no interruptions. Corporate says each 5-pack should take 90 seconds. Four crates per hour.

Hah!

I wish some ass from Corporate would come down here and demonstrate.

They want one hundred fifteen 5-packs out on the floor each day. That's twelve cases—cut, shucked, wrapped. It might be possible if someone besides me pitched in. Or if I were a robot.

The first day, Justus helped me for an hour. He chopped while I shucked. Slung a slogan at me, "By myself I make a difference, together we go the distance."

No lack of slogans around here.

Then he left the job to me.

Yesterday, right after I brought up twenty 5-packs, he stomps into Produce looking for more corn, complaining the displays aren't full.

"What if we go back to two displays, instead of three?" I say.

If the darts in his eyes were real, my face would be perforated.

"This is a display business, Sadie. I will never take down a display. Do you understand that?"

A vision flashes through my head: displays from Halloween, Christmas, Easter, destined to remain forever. I consider telling him to fuck himself and give his back the finger as he walks away from me. Remembering the omniscient security cameras, my finger quickly retracts.

"Excuse me, Justus?"

"What?"

"If I may make a suggestion, perhaps if there were two displays, instead of three, I could keep them full, and they'd look better."

He frowns and cocks his head, evaluating the situation. Evaluating me.

"Are you up to this job, Sadie?"

"I'm not sure."

"Why not?"

"My hands go numb at night."

He stares at me, as if I'm lying.

"That's not good," he says, his eyes calculating workman's comp. "I may have to move you to another department, but I don't have anything."

No offer to get me help. Just the threat of being fired.

"If you can't do this job—"

"I can."

"Then do it."

I've decided how to kill him.

That's wishful thinking, Sadie.

"NO IT'S NOT!"

I'm sick of being a masochist.

I stop pacing, stand by the sliding doors that lead out to my tiny balcony, listen to passing cars and the neighbor's dog that won't stop barking. A breeze slips through the screen door; the air smells of smoke. Forcing my numb hands to work, I slide the screen door open, step onto the miniscule deck. Up here, on the second floor, I have a fine view of the wooden fence and the road beyond it. I unfold the chair I found down by the dumpster. It wobbles, creaks when I climb onto the seat. Standing on the chair, I can see over the fence to the bike path that runs along this side of the road.

Passing cars streak by.

If I had a water balloon, I bet I could hit that Subaru.

Justus rides his bike along this path every morning on his way to work.

The pain in my hands has changed from burning to pins-and-needles. A good sign. It means they're coming back to life. I climb down from the chair, go back inside, and flop onto my bed. I lie on my stomach, my left arm dangling off the mattress. For some reason this helps to alleviate the tingling.

I've been reading up on sadomasochism. A masochist is passive and a sadist is active, but both traits can exist within one person. Really, a masochist and a sadist are part of a whole, like yin and yang, negative and positive, me and Justus.

I need to reframe my reality.

No more Sadie the Wimp, Sadie the Downtrodden, Sadie the Masochist.

I fall asleep listening to a self-help podcast about the power of positive thinking, and I feel positively positive about my transformation.

Recipe
Sadie's Hot Shit Brownies

Baking calms my nerves, and my favorite ingredient is chocolate. Chocolate hides a multitude of sins, so if you screw up a recipe no one notices. I always use dark chocolate, because it contains antioxidants. Antioxidants lower blood pressure and, since I started working at the supermarket, mine is rocketing.

This is my mom's recipe. She used to make brownies when my father was in a lousy mood, so she made them a lot—until the day she slit her wrists. (I found her in the bathtub.) My mom never added nuts, but I do—walnuts, pecans, whatever nuts I have on hand. If you like dark and intense, check these out.

Hot Shit Brownies

Ingredients:
¾ cup butter, melted
1 cup white sugar
½ cup brown sugar
3 eggs
2 teaspoons vanilla extract

1½ cup all-purpose flour

½ teaspoon salt

½ teaspoon baking powder

½ cup unsweetened cocoa powder

½ cup dark chocolate chips (Can also use part butter-scotch, white chocolate, or any shit you like.)

½ cup nuts, chopped

Preparation:

Preheat oven to 350 degrees Fahrenheit. Grease an 8x8 inch, square baking pan. Using a whisk, combine the melted butter, sugar and vanilla. Add eggs one at a time. Combine flour, cocoa, baking powder, and salt in another bowl. Add dry ingredients slowly to wet, stirring until blended. Stir in nuts, chocolate chips, etc. Spread batter into pan. Bake 30—35 minutes, or until tester comes out clean. Do not over bake. Cool before cutting—I know it's hard to wait! I recommend removing yourself from the kitchen. Time passes faster if you do something productive, like vacuum or masturbate.

GOING DOWN

I WAKE UP LATE, STAY IN bed sipping coffee and nibbling brownies—my hands so numb that I can barely hold the cup. They'll get better as the day goes on. After streaming a few episodes of *Deadly Women*, I stare at my ceiling, daydreaming. Then it's time for work.

I put on my uniform: black pants and the dreaded shirt we have to wear on Fridays. Banana yellow with tomato red letters running across the front and back, stating: *My Job is to Serve You!* On yellow shirt days, I feel like a billboard for masochists. I plan to cover *My Job is to Serve You!* with my apron and a sweater. I slap the company ball cap on my head, grateful that the brim hides my eyes.

I ride my bicycle to work, saves on gas, and I don't have to find a parking space. Employees aren't allowed to park cars in the store lot—we have to park in back, on a street that has no lights, and hope vandals don't destroy our cars.

I coast along the bike path, glance at the river. The water is green and kind of muddy, running slow due to lack of rain.

The sky would be clear blue, typical for Colorado in early July, but there are wildfires up north. The sun struggles to shine through gray haze, and smoke has settled on the mountains. I pedal past the science museum, past the library, past Happy Valley—the old folks' home. When I hit a hill, I have to pump and my lungs sting. So do my hands, but the familiar pain propels me faster. Today I'm eager to get to work, excited to see Justus.

THIS TOWN IS FULL OF bike fanatics, and the racks outside the store are crowded. A lot of people ride their bikes to work, like me. And Justus. But he doesn't use the bike rack. Because he's Assistant Manager, he gets to keep his bicycle downstairs in the meat locker.

I spot him as I enter. He's up front by the cut fruit case, inspecting the corn display. Six shelves, and four are empty. Each shelf holds twelve 5-packs. I do the math. I need forty-eight more 5-packs to fill the sucker—240 ears, so five cases. And that's just one display; there are two others.

But today I have a plan, and nothing brings me down.

I nod hello to Checkers and Courtesy Clerks as I pass them. Courtesy Clerks are the lowest of the low in the supermarket hierarchy. I know. I used to be one—then I got promoted to Salad Bar. Courtesy Clerks get paid less than anyone else. They bag groceries, run around the parking lot corralling shopping carts (people abandon carts in the bushes, behind the dumpster, by the bus stop), empty trash, clean bathrooms (including the disgusting *Men's Room*), and are generally bossed around by Checkers. Checkers are the supermarket rock stars. Once, when I was a Courtesy Clerk,

I referred to myself as a Bagger, and the CRM in charge corrected me: *Courtesy Clerk, not Bagger, Sadie.* But when I checked the company website, my job status said: *Bagger.*

By the way, CRM stands for *Customer Relations Management.* They're the people you see standing around watching the Checkers. The ones who look like they're not doing anything.

I clock in, smile at the woman behind the service desk.

"Have a great day, Doreen."

She eyes me suspiciously.

"Why're you so happy?"

"No reason."

I head toward the cut fruit and Justus. He's speaking to the Produce Manager, the head of my department. Maybe you didn't know this, but each department has a manager and an assistant manager. Justus, the Assistant *Store* Manager, is in charge of all the *department* managers, and the *Store Manager* is in charge of Justus. This place is full of bosses. The Produce Manager is a nice guy, consequently Justus spends a lot of time trying to *improve* him. They watch me as I approach, the Produce Manager smiling, Justus scowling.

Usually I'd feel nervous, but today I'm whistling along with the piped-in music. Everything I do here has a soundtrack. Right now it's "Never Rains in Southern California," a song I despise.

Justus zeros in on me.

"Chop, chop," he says as I walk past.

I imagine his head, bashed-in like a Jack-O-Lantern after Halloween.

Grinning, I turn back to him.

"I'll get right on it."

"How are your hands?" His tone sounds concerned, but his eyes bore into me, noting all my faults.

"Better," I lie. "The gloves help a lot."

After our little chat about corn, when he hinted he might fire me, he called me into his office for a *safety meeting* and gave me two flimsy wrist braces. At first he only gave me one, no doubt wanting to avoid too much of an investment, but I mentioned that I have two hands and finagled a second glove. They help a bit, but what I really need is less time spent shucking corn.

"Glad to hear it," he says now. "We need this display filled ASAP."

"Okay," I say, and head to the Salad Bar.

Low on lettuce and Ranch dressing; it could also use a refill on red onions and chick peas.

I glance at Justus, see him watching me.

I hurry past the new fake robot in Deli—part of the remodel. The thing doesn't move like a real robot. It stands stationary, has some kind of sensor so it speaks to people as they pass, "May I take your order? You can save a dollar."

"Fuck off."

Damned thing wants my job.

I sprint through the remodeled bakery, duck into the same old, dreary *Employees Only* area, and hit the button for the new freight elevator. Someone must be loading stuff downstairs. I keep hitting the button, even though I know it won't light up while the elevator is in use. I consider taking the stairs, but they're on the other side of Meat and Seafood, and I don't want to risk running into Justus again.

Not yet.

Next thing I know, he's standing next to me.

"You work this weekend, Sadie?"

Sadie the Sadist to you.

I like the way that sounds!

Can't help smiling.

"Yup, I work this weekend. You?"

"Going camping for the holiday. Three days off."

"That's nice." I punch the button.

"See how it's not lighting up? That means it's in use," Justus explains, as if I'm an imbecile.

I punch it one more time, for grins.

"The Olathe corn shipment arrived today, and Corporate expects big sales. Corn is our number one priority, so I need you to keep those displays filled. Understand?"

I use my cheery voice, "I'll be here, chopping away."

Justus presses the button, and this time it lights.

"When do you leave on your camping trip?" I ask.

"Tomorrow, early, but I'll be here till late tonight getting the store prepared for the holiday. July third is as busy as Christmas Eve."

I stare at my sneakers, thinking.

Say, "Be careful of those fires."

I hear the beeping sound, the rattle of the elevator. The door slides open, revealing the steel jaws and then the grill. Liam, a kid I work with downstairs, lurks behind a U-boat teetering with cartons of mushrooms, rutabagas, cauliflower, carrots. He hardly ever speaks, and now is no exception.

Justus ignores him, but I say, "Hi."

Wordlessly, Liam rolls the cart out and disappears onto the floor.

I enter the elevator before Justus, consider hitting the > < button to shut the door on him, but he's too fast.

He follows me inside.

"Stand back," he says.

As if I can't read the shocking pink warning sign.

Justus hits **B** and then > <.

He faces the door, his back to me.

I focus on his bald spot, skin pulled tight over his skull.

A target.

The door's jaws begin to clamp together. I count, *one chimpanzee, two chimpanzee, three*—measuring how long the process takes. Sometimes the jaws get stuck midway, and closing takes a bit longer, but usually they glide easy as chomping a ripe peach. If I pushed Justus, he would fall forward. If I push him *right now*, chances are, he'll put out his arms to brace himself. But, if I hit him hard enough, his head will lodge between those closing slabs of steel.

My hand stretches toward his back. And then I wonder, if his head is sandwiched between those jaws, will it set off an alarm? And won't the elevator stop moving? If that's the case, how will I get him downstairs and dispose of his body?

I pull back my hand.

"Too soon."

I guess I spoke out loud, because Justus turns to look at me.

"What's too soon?"

"Too soon for Olathe corn," I say. "Doesn't it usually come after the Fourth?"

I congratulate myself on my quick thinking.

Justus runs a manicured finger over his mustache, surprised that a peon like me is privy to such arcane knowledge.

"That's right, Sadie. The Olathe crop is early this year."

The elevator stops.

I follow Justus into Produce.

He points to a stack of black plastic crates filled with corn and wrapped with cellophane to hold them together.

"Grab an RPC. I'm going to show you how to chop."

"I know how to chop," I say, but he keeps pointing.

The crates are stacked so high, I need to stand on my tip-toes to pry one off. I tear away the cellophane and manage to move the crate on top. My wrists shake as I bring it down.

"Set it by the trash," Justus tells me as if I'm clueless.

"I need to double bag the can," I say, "so it doesn't rip."

If Justus thinks a single bag will be enough, he obviously has had very little experience with corn. The fact that he thinks he's some kind of expert is more than annoying.

My gaze falls on the machetes lined up on the magnet strip, immaculate and shiny after soaking in the chlorine solution I use for cleaning. I've been reading up online: Chlorine can remove visual evidence of blood, but to completely destroy hemoglobin, so it can't be detected by forensics, you need a cleaning agent like hydrogen peroxide. *Peroxy,* the stuff that squirts out of the power hose I use to mop this concrete floor. I'm the last one out at night, so that job falls on me.

I grab my guillotine and place it over the double lined trash can.

"Wrong way," Justus says, as if I'm some dummy. "Turn it around."

"I'm a lefty."

Justus raises an eyebrow, as if my left-handedness explains a lot of things.

To accommodate his superior right-handedness, he turns the guillotine around and unlocks the safety catch, allowing the arm to swing up. Then he grabs an ear of corn and aligns it with the blade.

"They call me the Colonel," he says, as he brings the arm down.

"The kernel, that's hilarious." I hand him another ear.

He repeats the process.

"You shuck, while I cut."

I want to take this ear of corn and shove it up his Type A ass.

Silently, I scream, *GO SHUCK YOURSELF.*

I draw gloves he gave me over my tingling hands and wrap the bands around my tingling wrists. Securing the Velcro a little too tightly, I imagine his neck.

Wait.

I pull on rubber gloves, careful not to get white powder on my black pants. I don't want to leave any prints.

But, instead of grabbing Justus, I reach for an ear of corn.

Disappointed in myself, I peel away the husk, revealing kernels the color of chicken skin.

The piped-in music plays "Take This Job and Shove It."

I sing along.

An announcement blasts over the speaker system: *Call for Justus on line two.*

He stops chopping.

"I'll be back later, check on how you're doing."

I shuck the ears that Justus cut—all six of them.

Impressive.

Itchy blotches creep along the inside of my forearms, crawl over my neck. I can't stop scratching. I read a blog called **The *Real* Children of the Corn.** The kid who wrote it says everyone working in the cornfields gets Corn Rash. He said it's caused by thousands of little razor cuts from the husks, but I suspect it's also caused by all the chemicals they use. Justus says this corn isn't genetically modified, but I know they spray it with all kinds of poison: one to kill the weeds, another so the crop survives the weed killer, something else for bugs and worms. It's a wonder we can eat this stuff. I watched this documentary, *King Korn,* and learned most corn grown in the

United States is inedible, not to mention unprofitable. The only way farmers make any money is government subsidies. The corn they grow is used to manufacture stuff like ethanol, high-fructose corn syrup, fillers in things like toothpaste and varnish. The two guys who made the film had their hair tested and it was composed mostly of corn.

Most Americans are mostly made of corn.

I need to chop more.

I wheel the trash over to my corner, so I won't be in anybody's way. Pull three more crates off of the stack and bring them to my area. I set up RPCs (reusable plastic containers): one for cut corn, one for shucked.

Chop, chop, chop.

I imagine Justus's pasty hand lying in between the blades, imagine his manicured fingernails trembling at the ends of his pale fingers.

I lower my guillotine and his hand falls into the trash.

The doors to Produce swing open.

Liam appears. He squeezes past a pallet loaded with crates of cabbages and broccoli, then disappears into the cooler. A minute later he rolls out a U-boat stacked with boxes of berries.

He nods at the RPCs I've carefully arranged on the counters by my sinks.

"More corn," he says, surprising me with his effusive speech.

"Corn is my life."

He shakes his head and leaves.

We both work the late shift and most nights it's the two of us and no one else. One time, as we both stood in the elevator waiting for the jaws to close, I mentioned it was like a giant mouth devouring endless crates of corn.

He said, "A soul-sucking mouth devouring employees."

I'd never heard him speak so many words.

Since then, I've felt we have a bond.

I wonder if he'd help me move the body. Shoving dead weight into the compactor will require more muscle than I can muster on my own, plus Liam's aversion to speech might prove to be an asset.

I keep chopping.

The music goes through a rotation: popular songs from the 1970s, '80s, '90s—hardly anything from the millennium we've been in for more than a dozen years. Now it's disco, Michael Jackson's "Don't Stop 'til You Get Enough," as if Justus is inside my head, commanding me to chop more corn.

Chop, chop, chop.

I ponder how best to dispose of his body.

After cutting two cases, it's time to dump the trash—more than two cases of cob bits, and I can't lift the bag. I roll the garbage can out of Produce, open the compactor's door—trying not to breathe the stink—heave the bag into the pit.

I double-bag the garbage can again.

As I start chopping yet another crate of corn, the solution occurs to me: *divide and conquer.*

No need to enlist help if I chop the body into pieces.

I glance at the clock, wondering when Justus will return.

Chop, chop, chop.

Shuck, shuck, shuck.

Wrap, wrap, wrap.

I've chopped, shucked, wrapped, six crates of corn. Now I'm working on prepping the Salad Bar for tomorrow. The counter is lined with containers filled with sliced cucumbers, shredded carrots, artichoke hearts, chick peas, beets.

I'm trimming broccoli.

I last spotted Justus up front when I left the break room after lunch. Around here, they call it lunch even if it's 6:00 PM.

Wanting to avoid him, I veered into Housewares and circled through Dairy.

My timing needs to be perfect.

I intend to ambush Justus after I take down the Salad Bar.

I'll lure him down to my domain, my corner by the sinks where I chop and cut. When he has his back to me, I'll whack him with the machete or stab him with a chef's knife. I haven't quite decided, but the knives are waiting by my cutting board where I'm working on the broccoli.

When he's dead, I'll stash his body on the floor behind the trash can so he's hidden. Then I'll pull the salad cart in front of the trash can to act as a barrier. There's a drain on the floor by the sinks, so cleanup should be fairly easy. The only snag I can imagine is Liam, but he'll be upstairs stocking vegetables.

Liam leaves at about 9:00. After that, the basement will be deserted—except for the guy in the meat locker, way down the hall. Most of the day crew will be gone, and the night stalkers won't arrive till eleven. Night stalkers live on coffee and energy drinks. They stock the shelves while the store is closed and leave at dawn. The point is, I'll have about two hours to myself down in the basement. After Liam's gone, I plan to fillet Justus (if not fillets, pieces: legs, thighs, wings), then I'll deposit the parts into trash bags (doubled to avoid leakage), and toss the bags into the compactor.

When I'm done I'll mop as usual, spray the concrete with the hose, use a squeegee to drive bloody water into the drain—

The Produce doors part, revealing Liam. Head bowed, he rolls a cart of packaged lettuce, spinach, various herbs, past my station, maneuvering between a U-boat stacked with carrots and a ginormous pallet of corn. He enters the cooler.

I place the cut broccoli into a container, secure the lid. My hands tremble as I peel tape from a roll. Shake harder as I slap the tape onto the lid of the container. All this thinking makes me nervous. Using a black marker, I label the tape with today's date, so I'll know when to pull the broccoli from the Salad Bar.

I figure, no one will miss Justus till he's due back from his camping trip. Even then, maybe they'll think he got caught in a wildfire—they're spreading fast.

What about his bicycle?

Someone is bound to notice it hanging out in the meat locker.

I'll ride it home.

The more I think, the more my hands shake.

My plot has holes.

A rattling noise makes me jump.

I turn toward the sound, knocking the container of beets off the counter. Crimson juice splatters the white wall, spills red onto the floor. I watch it ooze into the drain.

Liam rolls a U-boat out of the cooler, its wheels clacking on the concrete floor as he heads out of Produce.

I lean against the counter, so I'll remain upright, press my hands into the stainless steel to stop them from shaking. I stare at the garbage disposal, wondering if the motor is powerful enough to grind bones. Swallow a mouthful of puke.

The clock says 7:00, time for me to surface from the basement.

I step over crimson stains, avoiding the remains of beets, and tell myself I'll clean the mess after I take down the Salad Bar.

Or later ... when I clean the rest.

Leaning into my cart, I steady my wobbly legs. I roll the cart out of Produce and down the hall to the freight elevator, push the button again and again and again.

TAKING DOWN THE SALAD BAR is meticulous work, requires patience. Going too fast may lead to disaster—kidney beans lost in the tomatoes, sunflowers seeds hiding in the shredded cheese. First thing, I slip on fresh rubber gloves. Leftover lettuce and spinach is thrown away, so I stack those containers on top of each other. Then I set the tongs and serving spoons into the empty lettuce bin. The collection of salad dressings often looks like a child got hold of finger paints. Fridays are the messiest, due to happy hour, and this weekend is a holiday, so it's worse than usual. Using gobs of paper towels, I wipe away white, pink, yellow, and red oily smears.

From the corner of my eye, I notice Justus. He's hovering around Liam, his head wagging as he points at the fruit display.

Liam continues stacking oranges while receiving the lecture.

I focus on the Salad Bar, examining each item as I remove the containers to determine if something needs to be replenished or tossed. I have my favorites, like purple cabbage and green peas—the colors are so vibrant. And there are items I dislike. In my opinion, baby corn and pepperoni have no business on a salad.

A man marches over, glares at the half-empty Salad Bar, and then glares at the loaded cart.

"No more salad?"

"Sorry. We take it down at seven."

He points at my chest.

I look down at the red letters on my yellow shirt. A splatter of beet juice drips from the **S**. The rest of *SERVE* is covered by my apron.

The man barks, "Your job is to serve me."

Broiled on a bed of lettuce?

The man stomps over to the Deli counter as I reach for the bin of peas.

A voice startles me.

"What did that customer want?" Justus demands.

The bin slips from my hands and peas spill onto the floor. I watch green pellets scatter.

"He wanted a salad," I say, falling to my knees, as if I'm about to beg for mercy. Crawling around the Salad Bar, I attempt to scoop up wayward peas.

"And what did you tell him?"

"We close at seven."

"Did you mention we have salad kits?"

Justus sweeps his hand toward the far wall of the department, residence of ready-to-eat Cobbs and Caesars.

"I, ah—I forgot about the salad kits."

"Then I guess I'd better let him know."

"Sorry."

"I'll speak to you downstairs, Sadie."

Squishing several peas beneath his shoes, Justus heads to Deli and the customer.

Speak to you downstairs means *I'll see you in my office.* His office is down in the basement, not far from Produce. But I'll let Justus search me out and find me at my workstation.

That suits my plans.

Clenching my teeth, so I won't cry, I finish cleaning the Salad Bar. A tear plops onto the sneeze guard, and I swipe it with my gloved hand, leaving a smear of Ranch dressing. I promptly spray the glass and wipe away all evidence.

I took this job thinking it might be fun, thinking cutting fruit and vegetables all day would be low stress. But Salad Bar has proved to be more pressure than I can endure. I imagine Justus giving me my notice, imagine my mortgage coming due and I can't pay, imagine no money for groceries, electricity, gas, my phone—not even wireless. My life will be a barren waste. I figure there're two paychecks between me and the homeless shelter.

Tears roll down my face, drip from my chin, and rain into the bin of sliced cucumbers.

Stifling a sob, I push the salad cart toward the freight elevator. To stop the tears, I bite the inside of my cheek, so hard that I taste blood.

Sadie the Sadist doesn't cry.

I'm back in my corner, waiting.

Liam left a while ago, but I know Justus is still in the store. I checked the meat locker for his bike and saw it by the sausages.

I've been thinking about Sadie the Sadist, wishing I could be like her. Sadie the Sadist wouldn't feel jittery at the thought of seeing Justus, wouldn't panic at the sound of footsteps.

I've stocked the Salad Bar for tomorrow. I've washed the bins, the food processor, the utensils. I've wiped down all the counters, swept the floor, emptied the trash. I even cut another case of corn so it's ready to be shucked first thing tomorrow. The last thing I'll do is mop.

Now I'm sharpening the knives. Of course, Sadie the Sadist is a figment of my imagination, an imaginary friend, but the more I think about her, the more real she becomes.

I pick up a chef's knife, catch her reflection in the blade. She winks at me.

Sharpening knives isn't easy. My left hand tingles so much, I can hardly grip the chef's knife. Forcing my fingers around the handle, I draw the blade through the sharpener.

"Sadie."

My heart jumps.

I glance up.

Night is the only time the floor is clear of crates, so I can see across the room with no obstructions. Justus stands at the door, arms folded over his chest.

"Got a minute?"

He walks toward me.

"I need to finish—"

"What's our number one priority?"

"Umm—corn?"

"No, Sadie. Customer service."

"But you said—"

"Customer. Service. Is our number one. Priority." He enunciates each word as if I don't speak English.

Imagining his Adam's apple beneath the blade, I pull the chef's knife through the sharpener.

"Sadie—"

My gaze meets his.

Justus must read something in my eyes, because he grabs my wrist.

The knife slips from my hand, clatters when it hits the floor, and glistens on the beet-stained concrete.

"You need to mop," he says.

"I plan to."

Stooping, I reach for the knife.

So does Justus.

The blade slices my skin.

I stand slowly, stare at my thumb. Blood spurts from the gash, reminding me of the water fountain by the break room. I feel no pain, only amazement, as red runs down my wrist and drips onto the concrete, joining rivulets of beet juice.

I wonder how I'll ride my bike if I can't grip the handles, wonder how I'll murder Justus.

He grabs a wad of paper towels, presses them around my hand. His face looks green, but that may be the result of the fluorescent lighting.

"Why are you laughing?"

I shake my head. Didn't know I was.

The paper towels are turning dark.

When I stop squeezing, my thumb gushes.

"Keep pressure on it," Justus says.

Last thing going through my head before I conk out: *No more shucking corn.*

Recipe
Sadie's Anytime Fiesta Dip

In my opinion, any day that I don't have to work is reason to celebrate, and though this dip is great for parties, I encourage you to make it for any occasion. For example: you scored two weeks off with workman's comp, they fired the boss you hate, the neighbor's dog (that won't stop barking) got run over. Make life a celebration!

Fiesta Dip

Ingredients and preparation: each grouping is a layer of the dip. Go in order. I like to use a clear glass pie pan or square baking dish to display each layer's color. This recipe can easily be doubled.

Layer 1:
    3 cans of bean dip (jalapeño); yes, bean dip looks like baby caca, but it's high in fiber, and this dish disguises it.

Layer 2:
    3 ripe avocados, mashed
    ½ teaspoon salt
    1½ teaspoon garlic powder

¼ teaspoon ground pepper

2 teaspoons lemon juice

Layer 3:

½ cup mayonnaise

1 cup sour cream

1 package Taco Seasoning

Layer 4:

1 can sliced black olives

Layer 5:

1 small bunch of green onions, chopped

Layer 6:

1 tomato, cubed

Layer 7:

Shredded cheddar cheese

Note: Most people serve this with corn chips, but I've switched to sweet potato chips or raw veggies. Sadie the Sadist suggests, if someone you don't like has been invited to the party, smash their face into this dip and they'll come up looking like a Jackson Pollock painting.

BAGGING

IT'S BEEN RAINING. COOLED THINGS off and stopped the fires. Today the sky is clear and blue, the kind of day that makes me want to ride my bike from one end of the river trail to the other, or venture up the scenic highway into the mountains.

Instead, I'm back at work.

I brought Fiesta Dip and left it in the break room. But everybody's mad at me, because of the safety record. I ruined it. Before Justus attempted to amputate my thumb, the store *claimed* to be accident free for over eight hundred days. As a reward, every fifty days Bakery left a big cake in the break room. But now, thanks to my so-called accident, the store is back to square one. Truth is, people constantly get injured around here: lifting heavy boxes, moving overloaded carts, messing around with box cutters and knives. They *say* safety first, but what they mean is: No matter how badly you're hurt, *say nothing.*

Justus had to report the incident, because I bled all over him.

I got Workman's Comp, two weeks off with pay and the store covers the doctor's bills. The cut left a scar—on my thumb and on my psyche—but there's no hope for a settlement, because Justus claims the accident was *my* fault.

Liar.

It's my word against his, and I'm afraid if I say anything (like the lunatic attacked me) I'll be fired.

The good thing: no more corn.

The bad thing: I've been demoted to *Courtesy Clerk*. Less pay, less respect, and a lot more garbage.

They say Salad Bar is too much for me.

Maybe they're right.

Liam thinks I should hire a lawyer. He says I should sue. But, if I sue, I'll lose the job, and in this lousy economy who knows if I'll find another.

I used my break from work productively. It gave me time to think, time for Sadie the Sadist to incubate. The more I hang out with her, the more I realize how much we have common. For example, we're both concerned with justice—especially for little guys, the silent slaves who do your dirty work, like Courtesy Clerks, Hotel Maids, Dishwashers, Janitors.

Don't get me wrong, Sadie the Sadist and I have our differences—she's a righty. I'm a lefty. Slight variations in programming, otherwise we're identical. Except she's a maniac. By that I mean, she's a lot more outspoken than me, fearless. I admire her courage, but sometimes I wish she'd shut her mouth. Other times I flip the switch to autopilot, let her drive.

Like right now, she's bagging groceries.

Bagging's a bit slower since the accident.

The scar on my left thumb makes it difficult to open plastic bags, but the feeling in my hands is back—slight tingling in the tips of my fingers. Maybe I just don't notice the pain I used to feel, because I'm taking Dilaudid, synthetic morphine.

Have you ever noticed how much you use your thumbs? The cut made a lot of simple tasks challenging: drinking a cup of coffee, typing, texting, using the remote, masturbating.

Did you know lefties have higher IQs than righties?

Sadie the Sadist would argue that point. She says two hands are better than one and since your brain has two sides you might as well use both. She's teaching me to be ambidextrous. Video games help a lot. *Saint's Row: The Third* is the best—guns, grenades, rockets, swords, even chainsaws. I got a lot of practice using my right hand while I was recuperating. I hope being right handed won't make me stupid.

"Plastic work for you?"

The guy nods. Most people do.

Most people don't mind plastic bags, but some people are bag snobs. Even when I tell them our plastic bags are biodegradable (made from corn-based material), they insist I use paper, as if killing trees makes them superior, or they bring their own bags—trying to save the planet. I hate to tell them, but this planet is going to hell, regardless of paper or plastic. Pretty soon we'll all be robots.

I take pride in what I do: bag veggies separate from meat, lay bread gently on the eggs, keep cold things together. But, sometimes, if you piss me off, I poke a finger through the plastic wrap guarding your chicken and allow chicken blood to seep onto your peaches.

"Have a great day."

A woman rolls a cart, filled with groceries and a shrieking toddler, into Check Stand 9 where I'm bagging. The toddler waves a glitter wand at me, lets out a high-pitched wail. Oblivious to the screaming demon in her shopping cart, the banshee's mother unloads a head of lettuce, hamburger buns, popsicles, chips—a mishmash of items that I'll have to bag separately.

Wendy, the cashier, who's been talking to her pal at Check Stand 10, snaps to attention.

"Do you have your savings card?" she asks the customer, then flashes her winning smile.

"I've got it somewhere."

The banshee lets out another shriek.

"Be a good girl, Arboles," the mother says distractedly, searching for her card.

Her tepid warning has no effect on the little witch.

Who names their kid Arboles, anyway—a nothing town out in the middle of nowhere, population 280.

The mother fishes through her purse while Wendy sighs, juts out her hip. Wendy won't ring anything up until the savings card is scanned, because it starts a timer. As soon as that card number is entered she'll start pushing stuff along the belt, so fast I'll have to hustle to keep up. At the end of each week the times are calculated and the speediest checker wins prizes like frozen pizza, store brand ice cream, a five-dollar gift certificate. Wendy always wins.

The woman emerges from her purse, card in hand, and that's my cue.

"Plastic okay?"

I stand between two racks of bags, willing her to say *yes*. Plastic is much easier to load than those fabric bags the tree huggers lug into the store, but nothing irritates me more than paper. Paper bags slide off my racks and, if I manage to load them, I'm too short to see into them. Whenever people ask for paper, I want to shout, *Timber!*

I don't say anything, but Sadie the Sadist does.

Nudging me, she whispers, *Fuck her; use the plastic.*

Without waiting for the woman's answer, I flounce my plastic bags, preparing them for loading.

"Whatever works," the woman says.

Score for me.

And score for her.

I won't smash her buns.

The toddler taps her glitter wand on my head.

I stick out my tongue and I quickly retract it. (Sadie the Sadist did that.)

The kid scrunches up her nose.

"I don't like you."

"I don't like you either," I say quietly, so only she can hear.

The wand slaps me.

"Arboles, that's not nice." The woman glances at me, concerned. "You all right?"

"Fine."

When her mother turns away, I bare my teeth at Arboles and snarl.

Wendy is on a roll, pushing toilet paper, celery, shampoo, eggs, and milk along the belt so quickly that I experience a pileup. You might think bagging is easy, but I have to think fast. The nightmare is forgetting to give a bag to a customer. If I notice in time, I chase them through the parking lot. Otherwise, I have to bring the bag to the Customer Service desk. Do that often enough and I'll be written up.

Justus already gave me a verbal warning.

Which reminds me: I haven't seen him today.

That realization lifts my mood.

Humming along to the piped-in music ("Life in a War Zone"), I finish bagging the woman's stuff and load each bag into the cart, while attempting to avoid an attack of the witch's wand.

At least the little shit stopped shrieking.

When they leave, I ask Wendy, "You seen Justus?"

She juts out her hip. "Why? You miss him?"

I smirk.

So does she, playing it cool, but everybody knows Wendy has the hots for him.

"Now that you mention it," she says to me, "I haven't seen that man since Friday." Then, turning to her buddy at Check Stand 10, "You seen Justus lately?"

"I heard he called in sick."

Wendy frowns. "Maybe he walked."

Employees do that around here, quit without giving notice. One guy marched over to the manager, threw his apron down, and shouted, "I can't take it anymore." Then there was the girl who worked in Deli for two hours, went for a smoke and never came back. Don't forget the bakers—two middle-aged women who got into a fistfight in the middle of the night. Frozen baguettes make great weapons.

Note to self: *If the baguette gets bloody, just stick it in an oven and bake away the evidence.*

My point is, people come and go here faster than Louie CK (Sadie's favorite comedian) agrees to a blowjob.

But I don't think Justus would walk. He's a manager, enjoys pushing people around and makes good money. Why would he give that up?

I've got a hinky feeling about him.

"Sadie, you're staring into space."

I don't like being interrupted. My hinky feeling is replaced by anger.

A supervisor stands in front of me. Curly hair, a goofy smile that makes me want to punch her teeth. I haven't memorized all the CRM's names yet, so I read her tag: *Terri*.

Terri for terrible.

"I need a propane exchange. Sadie, will you get that, please?"

She phrases it like a question, but it's an order. I head to the service desk, get the key out of the drawer, then meet the customer out front where we keep tanks of propane. I unlock the storage unit, the sun beating down, so hot I wonder if the tanks of propane might explode. I know they're not supposed to, but what if the tanks got so toasty they burst? What if someone lit a match?

The customer's car pulls up to the curb. He hands me an empty tank, and I hand him a full one. At any given time, we have over a hundred five-gallon tanks on hand, about five thousand gallons of propane. That should be enough to incinerate this building.

I go back inside, replace the key in the drawer, and head to Check Stand 9, but someone else is bagging—a kid they hired yesterday.

Terri looks up from her clipboard, says, "Sadie, it's your turn to do carts."

Bitch.

Have you noticed how she picks on me? I wanted to enjoy the air-conditioning, and now I have to go outside again. The last thing I feel like doing is dragging carts around the sweltering parking lot.

My fists clench. Sadie the Sadist is on the verge of punching Terri's nose.

Stop!

Sadie can be impulsive, but sometimes it's best to wait, best to make a plan.

Unclenching my fists, I summon my sweetest voice and say, "Sure thing, Terri. I'll get right on those carts."

I slip on an orange safety vest, grab a leash to rope the carts so they won't roll away—and add *Terri* to my list.

Recipe:
Sadie's Basic Soup Stock

My favorite recipes include stews and casseroles. Comfort food. I especially like soup—it's easy to make and versatile. This is a basic recipe for stock. Enjoy it as it stands, or use it as a base. It freezes well. This recipe calls for chicken, but you can substitute beef, pork, or other meat. Experiment. Use what you have on hand. I'm a great one for economizing. Remember bones add flavor, so be sure to include them. Enjoy!

Basic Soup Stock

Ingredients:

Chicken, cut into 4-8 parts (or other cuts of meat)
¼ cup oil
5 carrots, coarsely chopped
5 celery stalks, including leaves, coarsely chopped
Ginger root, coarsely chopped
1 large onion, unpeeled and coarsely chopped
1 head of garlic, cut in half
1 large bunch of parsley or cilantro

Sprig of whatever herbs you have around (thyme, sage, rosemary)

White wine to taste, about 1 cup (for red meat, use red wine)

Water to cover the meat

Preparation:

Heat oil in a large stock pot. Add vegetables and ginger. Cook till brown, about 10 minutes. Add chicken, herbs, wine, and water to cover the chicken. Lower heat to medium. When stock boils, lower to simmer. Here's the important part: remove chicken after simmering ½ hour, cut meat from the bone, return the bones to the pot to simmer for about 4 hours—skimming off foam as it forms. Removing the meat ensures it won't be overcooked, returning the bones ensures that you'll get the flavor. After the stock has reduced, strain out the bones and vegetables.

After I make stock, I like to let it sit in the refrigerator overnight. That allows the fat to rise, so I can skim it from the surface. Leave a little fat for flavor. Ginger adds a kick, and sometimes I'll add a lemon, or a dash of cayenne. To make soup: cut up the saved meat and return it to the stock, add sautéed vegetables, barley or pasta—whatever you like, bring to a simmer, and season to taste with salt and pepper.

Note: This basic recipe can be doubled, tripled, quadrupled—depending on how much meat you have. It's a great way to get rid of leftovers. Make sure you pick out all the bones (the small ones can be sticklers) or they may be used as evidence.

SEX IN THE BATHROOM

OVER THE PAST FEW DAYS a lot has changed at the supermarket.

The check stands have been moved so the contractors they hired for the remodel can redo the floor, plus they've rearranged the aisles again. Bandages are no longer next to macaroni; you'll find them on Aisle 6 across from oatmeal.

There's this new guy in Deli. He's about my age, not a kid, but not an old man either. His glasses make him look intelligent and I like his legs. They're muscular and tan. I know, because he wears shorts to work. (We're allowed to wear black, knee-length shorts from Memorial to Labor Day.) I met him on the freight elevator. I was bringing down the trash cart, after emptying all the garbage cans, when Ranger rolled in a U-boat of roasted chickens destined for the dumpster. His name is Richard, but everybody calls him Ranger. He helped me load my garbage into the compactor—the bags from the trash cans outside the store are especially heavy—and, in return, I gave him a BJ in the employee bathroom. It's unisex, down in the basement, and the door locks.

Now the poor schmoe is in love with me. Women sense these things, and we lefties are intuitive. He's obsessed. I feel his eyeballs on my butt whenever I walk past.

But blowing Ranger is not the big thing (no pun intended). The big thing is: **Justus is dead, and I'm not sure if I killed him.**

I heard about the accident this afternoon, as soon as I arrived at work. Several versions spread through the store like wildfire. According to one account, a car hit him up on River Road, not far from where I live. Another says he suffered a heart attack while riding his bike to the supermarket. A third version claims a passing car spat a rock that hit him in the head.

Unlike me, Justus never wears a helmet.

Anyway, he's gone.

But I don't think it was an accident.

Cut to several weeks ago, when I was at home recovering from *my* so-called accident. (I call it Justus attempting to slice off my thumb.)

I live alone, thanks to my ex-husband. He wanted kids. I didn't. He used to bug me all the time. Irreconcilable differences, but we never divorced. I guess I should call him *late*, not ex.

The guy was far from punctual except when it came to dying. He croaked three years ago when he was thirty-one and I was twenty-nine. We bought this condominium, then one night when he was drunk (as usual) he took a bad fall down the stairs leading from our unit to the courtyard. They call them units, not apartments, which sounds like some kind of cell, but really the place is pretty nice: two bedrooms, one and a half baths, and a working fireplace. Anyway, he cracked his skull on the concrete and I inherited the mortgage. Also a used truck, my husband's power tools, and $30,000 life insurance from his job as a plumber. That's how I bought my Cruiser bike, smart TV, smartphone, iPad, a new laptop, I don't remember what else—but the money's gone. The truck guzzles gas, so most of the time I ride my bicycle.

Anyway, several weeks ago, after my so-called accident, I was hanging out on my balcony, sipping Diet Pepsi and popping Dilaudid while checking out the passing cars, when I spotted Justus on his bicycle. I tracked the bald spot on his head as he rode along the bike path, passing my condominium complex, kept watching as he cycled along the path and turned toward the supermarket.

That's when Sadie the Sadist convinced me to start practicing.

The bandage on my left hand made climbing down from the folding chair difficult, so I had to support myself with my right hand. That's how the whole ambidextrous thing started. After climbing down, I noticed something annoying in my shoe, took the shoe off and found a pebble. Using my right hand, I threw the pebble off the balcony. Not a bad shot. I managed to hit the wooden fence, and I felt sure, with practice and a heavier object, I could hit a passing car—or bicycle.

"Sadie, you're staring into space again."

Terri the Terrible glances at her clipboard.

"It's 7:45. You're scheduled to clean the bathrooms. Make sure you sign off, and don't forget to mop the Men's Room."

"Will do."

My foot juts out; Sadie the Sadist is about to trip Terri, but I quickly pull back my sneaker (Nike, *Air Pegasus*—understated, classy).

Sadie the Sadist is disgusted.

Wimp.

"Shut up."

A customer glances at me, no doubt wondering if *shut up* was meant for her.

"Sorry, ma'am."

I meander toward the bathrooms.

During the day the store hires a porter, but come evening cleaning is the responsibility of Courtesy Clerks. The Men's Room is always gross; talk about needing practice taking aim.

Before hitting the bathrooms, I detour through Pharmacy and circle the store's perimeter, passing through Dairy, Meat, Bakery and Produce to reach Deli.

I spot Ranger by the display of roasted chickens. This time of day, they pull leftover chickens and throw them in the compactor.

The fake robot senses my approach.

"May I take your order?"

"Shut up, stupid."

"What?" Ranger looks up from the case, pokes his glasses.

"Not you, the robot."

Ranger smiles and I smile back.

"You due for a break soon, Ranger?"

"After I dump these chickens."

"Meet me in the Men's Room in ten minutes."

His smile gets wider. "Sure thing, Sally."

My grin shatters.

"Sadie," I correct him.

He appears confused.

"My name is *Sadie*."

"Sadie, right." He turns his attention to the chickens. The bags they're wrapped in are different colors: Yellow for Lemon Pepper, green for Sage, red for Barbeque. "Sorry."

I say, "It's okay."

But it's not.

I stand there, watching Ranger, ideas formulating.

He glances at me. "What?"

I don't like his condescending tone of voice.

"Nothing."

"I said I'm sorry."

As if that excuses him.

When I was off work, due to the *accident*, I had a lot of time to read. Not only self-help, other things. I downloaded a few books, including *Cereal* (by Blakette Crotch and Josephine Kornrash), about this woman who works in a supermarket, like me. She has this thing for Raisin Bran. I think it's a true story. Anyway, I found it inspiring.

I bat my eyelashes at Ranger, imagining how he'd look completely naked, his skin oiled and brown, juices flowing as I roast him slowly on a spit.

"You're a sweet girl, Sadie."

"No I'm not."

He places the color-coded bags on a cart, preparing to dump them. Says, "There are starving people in this world who'd kill me for these chickens."

"In this town," I add. "So, are we on?"

"I could go to hell."

"For fucking me or dumping chickens?"

I walk away, feel him watching my posterior. I think of *his*, tight and muscular.

Pausing by a display of salami, I lean over the bin, admiring the sausages, and twerk my ass for Ranger.

I'm gratified when I hear the splat of roasted chicken falling on the floor.

A sudden craving for corn—the food I've been avoiding, find repulsive—steers my body into Produce. I grab an ear out of the bin—big, fat Olathe—and slip it into a pocket of my apron. The store has cameras everywhere, but at this time of day the security guy is probably half-asleep, bored out of his mind from staring at monitors. I pass through Dairy, shove a tub of imitation butter into another pocket.

Rack it up to *shrink*; that's supermarket jargon for losses.

I circle back to the bathrooms, collect a spray bottle of cleaner and a box of paper towels from the cart sitting at the entryway, pull on rubber gloves, and push open the door marked *Women's*.

A customer washes her hands at the newly refurbished sink, oblivious to the mess she's making. Drips of soap smear the counter and water spills onto the floor. She glances at me and, noticing my cleaning supplies, offers a patronizing smile.

"I'll get out of your way," she says politely, but disdain screams from her eyes.

"No hurry, take your time." Under my breath, Sadie the Sadist adds, "Meanwhile, I'll fill that sink with soap and you can lick it clean or die."

I don't think the woman heard me.

She waves her hand at the automatic dispenser (another recent upgrade), wipes her hands on the resulting towel, and tosses the crumpled paper at the trash can. She doesn't notice (ignores it) when the towel lands on the floor.

I wonder what would happen if I spray this cleaning solution in her eyes. Would the whites turn red? Would the ammonia burn? Cause a milky film to form on her retina? Would she beg me to stop?

The woman leaves. I squirt the counter, wipe it. After polishing the mirror, I run my gloved fingers through my hair, mouse brown, nondescript. I wonder how I'd look if I dyed it flaming red. Red is an appropriate color for Sadie the Sadist, don't you think? I turn sideways to the mirror, stand on tip-toes, suck in my gut. The tub of imitation butter pouches my apron, and I look like I'm about to give birth to an alien. I slip my hand into the apron's pocket. The cob of corn feels like a giant hard-on.

Makes me think of Ranger.

I glance at the stalls. Chances are *Terri the Terrible* will come in here to inspect my work, so I *have* to clean the toilets. I pull my phone out of my pocket (we're not supposed to carry phones, but everybody does), check the time, and realize I'd better hit the Men's Room if I want to hook-up with Ranger.

Thinking about his ass makes me cream.

I fill out the chart taped to the door of the Women's bath-room. Time: 8 PM. Cleaning: visual, light, or deep. (I choose deep.) Initials. Hugging the spray bottle and box of paper towels, I head to the Men's Room, anticipation causing pussy juice to trickle down my thighs.

I knock, and then call out, "Anybody in there?"

No answer, so I push the door open.

A guy stands at the urinal, shaking himself.

"Be right out," he says.

I watch as he zips his fly.

Bypassing the sink, he leaves.

Do men ever wash their hands?

I set the *Cleaning/Wet Floors* sign outside the door. To pass the time while I wait for Ranger, I spray down the counter, glance into the stalls. One's not too bad, but the other looks like a ticker tape parade marched through it: streamers of shitty toilet paper trampled on the floor. I'll leave that mess for the porter.

I glance at my phone, checking the time.

Ranger should be here by now. Dumping chickens shouldn't take twenty minutes. I go out to the cleaning cart to get the mop and pail of water, glance toward the check stands.

No sign of him, so I text: *Wair r u?!?*

I watch my phone for a full minute.

No response. So, I call him.

Finally, he picks up.

"What? I'm working."

"Are you coming?"

"Later."

"Hahaha."

What does *later* mean? Before I have a chance to ask, he hangs up.

If he's not coming, I'll come by myself.

I grab the mop and dunk it into the pail, splashing water on my sneakers. The Men's Room floor is covered with yellow-brown foot prints. I mop around the toilets, avoiding strands of paper, and back my way out of the door.

I had plans.

I hate it when someone screws up my plans.

The dent in my female pride deepens into a chasm—a dark abyss churning with rage.

I bend over the pail and twist the mop, imagining it's Ranger's neck, imagining it's every man who's ever jerked me around. The corncob in my pocket jabs me, and wet heat rushes through my body as I formulate a *new* and *better* plan. The thought of it makes my slit gush.

Forget the Men's Room. I need privacy.

I run back to the door marked *Women*, peeling off my rubber gloves. All the stalls are empty. *Good.* I duck into the first one, secure the lock. Bending over the pail meant for discarded tampons, I quickly shuck the cob of corn, dig my fingers into the tub of margarine and butter up. I'm dripping with anticipation. The cob slides right in.

Who doesn't love creamed corn?

I GET OFF AT 9 PM (no pun intended). Ranger gets off at 10. (I mean that *literally*.)

Before I clock out, I hit the Deli again. Ranger's wiping down displays. Admiring his butt, I watch him bend over the glass. After a few moments he notices me.

"Sorry, Sadie. I couldn't break away."

"Couldn't or wouldn't, *Richard*?" I call him by his real name to let him know I'm pissed.

"Don't be mad. I'll make it up to you."

Yes, you will.

"Okay, Dick. Meet me at the river when you're done. By the picnic tables." It's not a question, not even an invitation. It's a command.

He swipes the glass before saying, "Sure."

Softening my tone, I say, "We'll have fun. I'll bring vodka." And then I flash a smile.

"Okay. See you in about an hour."

His shoulders drop about three inches as he relaxes.

My plan is falling into place, only a few more details I need to take care of.

I cruise past the check stands. It's all self-checkout at this hour, so they don't need baggers, I mean, *Courtesy Clerks*. I have plenty of other duties to occupy my time: emptying trash, restocking bags, cleaning check stands, returning shop-backs to their proper place, and there's always conditioning the shelves.

Wendy is working self-checkout. And the security guy is standing by, checking *her* out. Everybody knows (except the security guy, apparently) that Wendy's hung-up on Justus, so she's all upset about the accident. (Overly dramatic, if you ask me.) Anyway, I doubt the security guy will score anytime soon. Earlier today, I asked Wendy if she knew when they were holding Justus's funeral. She shouts, "That isn't funny, Sadie!" Then she broke into tears, abandoned her check stand, and stomped into the break room—like I'd said something weird. Wendy's been in the break room a lot today, sobbing on the couch; that's why mascara is running off her chin. But the security guy is oblivious, sniffing around her like a dog, hoping to find fertile ground where he can plant his boner.

Personally, I'm glad the dude is occupied, so he won't notice me. But, even if he's busy monitoring Wendy rather than the store, the cameras keep recording. I'm pretty sure I'm safe. He won't watch hours of nothing happening. A missing ear of corn will never be detected, and swiping a tub of fake butter is hardly a felony, but lifting a bottle of sleep aids might be noted, and in hindsight a missing bottle could be used as evidence. Receipts can be traced; I learned that from *CSI*.

Walking the aisles of Pharmacy, I condition bottles and boxes of various over-the-counter drugs, so I look like I'm doing my job. Conditioning involves pulling items forward, at least two deep, and lining them up for a waterfall effect. I zero-in on a bottle of Unisom Maximum Strength SleepGels. Turning my back to the camera, I slip the box into my apron.

Check my phone.

Time to meet Ranger.

Terri stands behind the Customer Service counter typing entries into a computer.

"I'm outta here," I say as I punch my code into the time clock.

Without looking up, she says, "You got the bathrooms?"

"Yeah."

"And the trash?"

"Uh-huh," I lie. I forgot about the trash.

After clocking out, I pick up a jar of cranberry juice. It takes me a while to find it, since they moved juice from Aisle 6 to Aisle 4, plus I got sidetracked because several people asked me where to find spaghetti sauce, pickles, croutons. I choose the store brand juice, so my purchase qualifies for the employee discount, and pay for it at self-checkout. I always use self-checkout. Interacting with human checkers requires more effort.

Then I head to the break room, glad to find it empty. I close the door. ME TV is on the new flat screen TV we got as part of the remodel. An ancient episode of *I Dream of Jeannie* competes with Elvis Costello singing "Allison" over the intercom. I open the jar of juice, take a few gulps, then dump about half of it into the sink. I'll spring for vodka at the liquor store. It's an investment, but Ranger will be worth it. I sit at the table where we eat lunch, push someone's forgotten container of chicken bones out of the way, and notice the latest *Gazette*. My hand shakes when I pick up the newspaper. A photograph of Justus stares at me from the front page. If I actually read the article and learn the details of his death, chances are I'll go into convulsions. I set the paper at the far end of the table, cover his face with chicken bones.

My hands tremble so badly, I have trouble opening the Unisom. I dump about a dozen SleepGels onto the table.

Using the box cutter they gave me when I worked in Produce, I slice into a pill and nearly cut myself. I breathe deeply, forcing myself to focus on the task, and squeeze the gelcap's contents into the jar of cranberry juice. I repeat the process fourteen times.

The door opens, and I quickly slip the bottle of Unisom into my apron.

"I thought you left a while ago," Terri says.

"Just collecting my stuff." I point to the half-empty jar of cranberry juice. "Needed to hydrate before riding home."

She sits across from me, pushes aside the container of chicken bones, and picks up the newspaper.

"So weird about Justus," she says. "I can't believe it."

"Heart attack?"

"No. Says here, 'possibly an accident.'"

"What does that mean, *possibly?*"

Terri reads aloud, "'Police continue to investigate.'" She glances at me. "You look flushed. Are you all right?"

"Just tired."

Preparing to leave, I reach for my helmet.

Nose back in the paper, Terri mumbles, "Guess they'll be looking for a new Assistant Manager."

"You applying?" I ask.

"Hadn't thought about it. Maybe."

I strap on my helmet, thinking about how I'd like to take this jar of cranberry juice and smash Terri's head. But that would put a damper on my plans.

"So," I say, "what, exactly, are the cops investigating?"

"The cause of the accident. It may have been a hit and run, or even intentional. Says here, 'Police are canvassing the neighborhood for possible witnesses.'" Her eyes meet mine, and the contents of my stomach lurches back into my mouth.

To keep it down, I take a swig of juice. "You live on River Road, don't you, Sadie?"

THE RIVER RUNS BEHIND THE supermarket, just across the road. At night, the road is dark and there's hardly any traffic. The city owns the strip of land along the river, so there are no buildings here—just scrub oak, sage, and brush. A steep path runs down the hill, leading to the picnic table where I wait for Ranger, earbuds plugged into my phone, listening to *Imagine Dragons*, one of my favorite bands; I love "Demons" and "Radioactive."

"Over here."

I wave the jar of cranberry juice as Ranger makes his way along the path. No moon tonight, but there's a haze of light from the supermarket. I've been taking nips of cranberry juice and vodka, and the diphenhydrAMINE (the active ingredient in Unisom) has started to kick in. I'm having a bit of trouble keeping my eyes open, and some difficulty focusing. For example, when Ranger arrives at the picnic table and sits next to me, I know he's real, but when I look at his face, then glance away, I see trails—like he's a ghost.

He removes the jar from my hands, downs a hefty slug and wipes his mouth.

"Tastes strange. What's in it?"

"Vodka and cranberry. Drink. You need to catch up."

He takes another gulp, and so do I.

We sit, listening to the river.

He tries to plant his lips on mine, but kissing feels too personal, so I avert my face.

"You feeling it?" I ask.

"Feeling what?"

I think he's worried. He thinks I want him to say, I love you, or some other shit.

"It," I say. "Are you feeling it?"

I clamp my hand over his crotch, squeeze his bulge.

My plan is working.

"Drink up, Ranger."

Even in my stupor, I can tell the drug is having an effect on him. His eyes are half-closed. They reopen when I drag down his zipper with my teeth, open wider when I take him into my mouth. There's a medicinal taste in the back of my throat and I try to get rid of it by sucking him in deeper.

Stroking the base of his cock, I move up and down, careful not to scrape him with my teeth. With the other hand, I cup his balls, feel them tighten. He tastes like salt and smells of musk.

He's groaning, and I'm afraid he's gonna come too soon.

"Don't stop, Sadie."

"Be right back."

I remove my yellow *My Job is to Serve You* shirt, yanking it, so the collar rips. (Earlier, I helped the rip along with a nick from my box cutter.) Then I tear off my bra. Ranger reaches for me, and my nipples tense. Leaning toward him, I press my tits around his cock. I've got his full attention now.

"You like this, Dick?"

"My name is Ranger."

"You're the Lone Ranger, aren't you, Dick?"

He moans.

"Any family?"

"My folks live in Albuquerque. You?"

"My dad's in Phoenix. I guess we're both loners here."

I lick his hardtop. His body arches backward, elbows pressed into the picnic table as he comes. A fountain of jism spurts all over me: my chest, my face, my hair. I make sure it hits my shirt, so I won't lose any evidence.

Sweat is pouring down his face.

He's groaning, but not with pleasure. He bends forward, clasping his head with his hands.

"I don't feel too good, Sadie."

"You need another drink."

He takes a few gulps, his eyes closed, his face flushed.

"I think I should go home."

"We're just getting started. I'll play some music." I plug my phone into his ears and blast "Blurred Lines."

"That song is sick, Sadie."

"That song is awesome, Dick."

He tries to stand, loses his equilibrium, plunks down on the bench.

"I gotta go now," he says, slurring. "I reaaally gotta go."

He stands again, his body swaying.

"Turn around," I order him.

When he doesn't move, I grab his shoulders, forcing him to turn. He's so blasted, it's easy to make him bend over the picnic table. I pull his shorts down to his ankles.

"What are you doing?"

"Blurred lines."

I slap his butt.

He attempts to turn toward me, but the shorts strangle his ankles and make him stumble.

He's loose as a ragdoll, my puppet. I turn him back toward the table, make him step out of the shorts.

"Spread your legs."

I shove my hands between his thighs, prying them apart.

His torso dives forward and his head clunks on the table. It's difficult to keep him upright, but the bench acts as support. His butt juts toward me, and I admire its smooth surface.

I reach into my apron pocket and pull out the cob of corn. It's already buttered. With one hand, I spread his cheeks, with the other I jab the cob. The hole is tight. Glad I brought the imitation butter, I scoop a handful and work one finger, then two, then three, inside of him.

My fist wakes him up.

When he yells, I pull out the box cutter and nick his balls—just enough to silence him.

"Keep yelling and your balls are history."

He retches, tries to shake me off.

Adrenaline courses through my body, gives me superhuman strength. With one hand, I hold the box cutter against his flaccid cock, while my other hand rams the corncob up his ass. I perform this feat with amazing dexterity, my practice paying off.

He's quiet now, his head glued to the table, glasses crushed and lying in a pool of vomit, the corncob slick with blood and shit.

I need to get rid of evidence pointing to his rape, but if I throw the cob in the river it will float, and if I bury it some animal may dig it up.

"Ranger." I tap him on the shoulder. "Ranger, you awake?"

No answer.

I attempt to lift him by the shoulders, but he's dead weight. Lying on the bench, I wriggle my feet under him and try to flip him over. His eyelashes flutter. I grab his hair, jerk up his head, and his mouth flops open. I shove the cob between his lips.

"Eat it."

Mechanically, he bites, then spits kernels onto the table.

I grab the cob, forcing it back into his mouth.

"Chew."

A jab from my box cutter encourages him.

"Swallow."

I turn the cob methodically, forcing him to eat every kernel.

When he's done, I let him sleep.

I take the cob down to the river, let the water wash it clean. Cars pass on the main road, but no one comes down here.

I feel at peace.

But I still have work to do.

I have to make this look good.

I pull my pants down around my ankles, squat on the bank, listening to the rush of water as I shove the cob into my cunt, sliding it in and out until I come, so hard that my eyes fill with tears. Then I sit on the corn, forcing the cob into my butt.

I'm bleeding, crying.

Perfect.

I wipe myself with the yellow shirt and pull up my pants.

For a long time, I stare at the river, watching how the water jumps around the rocks and keeps going.

Ranger is snoring.

I find the box cutter and run it over my chest. Not too deep, just enough to draw blood so it drips onto the table. I take Ranger's hand and press his fingers around the box cutter, making sure to leave a clear print.

Then I call 911.

Recipe:
Rockin' Rocky Mountain Oysters

What are Rocky Mountain oysters? Testicles. Usually the testicles of young bulls, but you can use whatever balls you have on hand, or in hand as the case may be: sheep, lamb, turkey, whomever—keep in mind the younger the testicles the more tender the oysters. Soak the balls in water, peel, and wash. In the olden days, cowboys sat around a campfire and tossed the testicles onto a hot griddle, cooking the balls until they exploded.

Warning: Many cultures say eating genitalia has an aphrodisiac effect, so these oysters may make you horny.

Rocky Mountain Oysters

Ingredients:
  2 pounds of testicles
  6-pack of your favorite beer (2 cans for soaking, 4 to drink)
  2 eggs, beaten
  1 cup flour

¼ cup corn meal
Milk
Salt
Pepper
Garlic powder
Canola Oil (or whatever fat you have on hand)
1 tablespoon hot sauce

Preparation:

If you have time, freeze the testicles—it's easy to peel them as they thaw. If they're fresh, you'll need a sharp knife to cut off the tough muscle. After the balls are peeled, toss them into a bowl of beer for two hours.

Add vinegar into a pot of boiling water. Parboil balls for a few minutes, drain, rinse.

While the oysters cool, mix together eggs, flour, cornmeal, salt, pepper, garlic powder. Season oysters with salt and pepper. Roll each oyster in the flour mixture, dunk into milk, then back into flour mixture. For a thicker crust, repeat.

Heat oil in a large pot, add hot sauce. Fry oysters until golden. Drain on paper towels. May be served with hot sauce, cocktail sauce, tartar sauce, or whatever you enjoy.

THE QUIET LADY

I'M NOT A VICTIM, I'M a survivor. That's what the trauma counselor told me when I went through the exam. They collected evidence for a rape kit, treated me for STDs and injuries, even drew blood to test for date rape drugs. I wonder if Unisom qualifies. In any case, there's enough evidence to convict Ranger, no matter what he claims.

But he doesn't remember much.

Out of the goodness of my heart, I didn't press charges. The district attorney is disappointed. There's not much she can do without me, because Ranger has no priors and there are no witnesses. I told her I'm not pressing charges, because I was horny and wanted to get laid. She says I'm suffering from shock.

In any case, Ranger will never stand me up again.

As a new employee, he was on probation for three months. Due to this incident, they fired him. It's a small town, so I don't think he'll find another job. Around here a rapist stands out. I heard he's returning to Albuquerque. They have lots of rapists there.

My one regret: not killing him.

Meanwhile, I'm laying low, spending time alone. I get enough of people at work, so on my days off I usually hunker down with a good book. (Right now I'm reading several, including *The Power of Now* by Eckhart Tolle and *Dark Nights of the Soul* by Thomas Moore.) When I'm too tired to read, I stream shows on my smart TV. *Breaking Bad* is my favorite. Walter White experienced a dark night of the soul, don't you think? But he managed to get out of it. At heart, I'm a scientist like Walt; I like to experiment. Cooking is chemistry. I've thought about following Walt *aka* Heisenberg's example and becoming a meth cook, but there's a lot of competition in that field. I think robotics is a better option.

Like I said, I spend a lot of time alone, *thinking*. But lately I've been hearing from people I haven't seen for a long time. The story of my rape made the *Gazette*. People I haven't heard from for a million years call to see if I'm okay—really, they want to hear the juicy details.

That's why I'm here at The Quiet Lady Tavern, waiting for Krista and Tracy. We used to hang out together before I got the job at the supermarket. I ran into Krista on the street. She volunteers at Safe Haven for Women, and she insisted that the three of us go out for happy hour. I happen to have two days off (Friday and Saturday—a rarity), and she caught me off guard, so I agreed to meet them. This morning I almost cancelled, then I decided going out would make me seem normal. I mean, that's what normal women do when they've been traumatized; they hang out with girlfriends, don't they?

I don't know.

Lately I feel removed from the human race. I feel like I need to wipe my hard drive clean and reboot. I think Sadie the Sadist has been tinkering with my programming while I sleep.

Anyway, thanks to Krista and Tracy, I'm sitting in a dim corner of The Quiet Lady, tapping my fingers on this table set beside a potted palm, when I realize: the cops took my fingerprints. My knee starts shaking and I order it to stop. The police told me the fingerprints were strictly for elimination purposes. But having my prints in the system means next time I'll have to be more careful.

I take a hefty gulp of the house red I ordered. *Tastes like acid.* I gaze into the wine. *Looks like blood.* I set down the glass, careful to place it in the center of the cocktail napkin, a challenge because now my hand is trembling. My knee shakes so hard it slams into the table. I check my phone. No calls. No texts. Krista and Tracy should be here any minute. I arrived early, hoping to get this spot. From where I sit, I can see the entrance, the bar and all the other tables. The potted palm provides a barrier, making me feel safe. To calm my nerves, I pop a Dilaudid (left over from the thumb accident) and peer into the vial. Still about a dozen pills, no refills. Maybe I should see that shrink again. After the rape, they had me talk to someone at Safe Haven. Maybe, if I ask her, she'll write me a prescription for something really good. She said I'm suffering from post-traumatic-stress disorder, that's why I'm so jittery.

Sometimes I wonder if I really *was* raped.

I take another sip of wine. Pick up the menu, try to read the shaking words, and set it down.

I remind myself to breathe. That helps a bit.

I think *women* make me nervous. They tend to talk too much. If I get another shrink, I want a man. Men don't talk.

I like The Quiet Lady. The atmosphere is Victorian, mahogany bar and fixtures, dim lighting. So dark it's kind of creepy. As you enter, you pass a marble statue of a woman. She has no head. That's why she's quiet.

My gaze travels across other tables—filled with the after work crowd and tourists—moves to the bar, and comes to rest on a loudmouth bitch. She'd look better without a head. A man, sitting on the stool next to her, notices me watching. He points at me, blows a kiss and laughs.

I glance at my phone. Text Krista: *i m hear.*

Get back: *Parking.*

Probably a brand-new Lexus.

Tracy arrives before Krista, not a surprise since Krista is always late. I met them a few years ago at the art center where I used to model. Life drawing class. Earned some extra money and I get off on people seeing me naked.

"Sadie, is that you?"

"I think so."

"You don't look like you. What happened to the cute, all American girl next door?"

"Dyed my hair to match my blood. I'm going for vampire."

I laugh, but Tracy doesn't.

"You look pale," she says. "Tired."

Bitch.

"You doing Botox or Restylane?" I ask.

"What?"

Tracy frowns, but her face barely moves.

She's older than me, but I have to admit, she looks good. *Well preserved.* She's wearing skinny jeans that must make breathing difficult, high heels, and a tangerine orange sweater, probably by some designer whose name I can't pronounce. When I'm with her, I feel the need to make excuses for my clothing. Except my sneakers; like most people in this town, I've got a thing for athletic shoes. Today I'm wearing Nike

Dual Fusion Run 2s, my usual black yoga pants and a purple tee-shirt from Wal-Mart.

Tracy looks me over. Doesn't mention my cool shoes.

I wonder how her head would look floating in formaldehyde.

"What was that snide comment about Botox and Restylane?"

"I *said*, are you doing a detox; you look rested."

"No, I'm not doing a detox. In fact, I need a drink." Still frowning, Tracy perches across from me as if she might take off any moment. She works for the *Gazette*, advertising sales, and patience is not her greatest virtue. Remembering that I'm a victim of rape, her tone changes, as if she's dealing with a difficult client, "Red hair suits you, Sadie. *Really.* And red is the hot color this fall."

"That's me, always on top of fashion trends."

Tracy glances around the tavern, eager to find a waitress. "I'm dying for a daiquiri; they're making a comeback, you know. How's your dating life?"

"Aside from being raped?"

"Sorry." Tracy's face turns the color of my hair. "That must have been awful."

Tracy's twice divorced, once from an accountant and, more recently, from a plastic surgeon. Her lifestyle demands a husband with a substantial paycheck. My needs, on the other hand, are simpler.

"I'm looking for a guy who's into power tools and asses."

"Me too." Tracy's Botoxed face reflects a modicum of interest. "I'd love a guy who's powerful and into assets. How do you plan to meet him?"

"I'll know him when I see him, stalk him for a while, then move in for the kill."

"That's my technique," Tracy says. "eHarmony or Match?"

"Home Depot."

Tracy manages to flag down the waitress and the girl—probably a college student judging by her straight, white teeth—takes her order. Teeth reveal a lot about a person. I run my tongue over mine and realize I need to brush. Floss too. Lately I've been using bleach strips, and I've noticed some improvement. I pick up my glass of wine then quickly set it down. I should have ordered white; the red may leave a stain.

"Hi, guys!" Krista waves as she walks toward our table, moving past the quiet lady without even a glance.

Sometimes I see her at the gym. She works out and so do I. I take spin and kick-boxing classes, lift weights, do the rowing machine and elliptical. I'm building strength and endurance.

Krista sits between me and Tracy, the only space available due to the potted palm. She's wearing spandex cycling clothes, and a Pearl Izumi windbreaker. She's blond and bouncy, has a husband who's a lawyer.

She gives me a concerned smile. Her voice is saccharine, or should I say stevia-tized? (Krista wouldn't be caught dead eating artificial sweetener.)

"How are you doing, Sadie?"

"Fine."

Impulsively (who cares if my teeth turn pink?), I drain my glass and motion to the waitress for more wine.

"I mean, *really*. Are you seeing a counselor?"

There's no stopping Krista. She's a do-gooder. Sometimes bitchiness is easier to handle. I wish Tracy would say something nasty.

"I saw a counselor at Safe Haven," I say to get Krista off my back.

"Wonderful! We have lots of good people there."

"I doubt *good* people can help me."

"Of course, they can. Think positive."

My knee is shaking overtime.

"What I need is a good butcher—"

Krista and Tracy have moved onto the topic of appetizers: baked brie or popcorn shrimp. I vote for Rocky Mountain Oysters.

"Sheep balls? Yuck." Tracy sticks out her tongue.

"My husband eats those things." Krista rolls her eyes. "Guess he thinks it's manly."

Ignoring me, they turn back to the menu.

"Ahi on a bed of greens sounds good," Krista says.

Meanwhile, I'm thinking about balls, the texture and chewiness. They taste a bit like liver. Add a few herbs, a little sherry, a whirl around the blender, and I think they'd make a fine substitute for pâté.

"I need someone who can show me how to take a body apart."

Tracy and Krista turn their attention to me.

"The Art Center is offering an anatomy class," Tracy says. "I thought you just modeled. I didn't know you're into art."

"Sculpture mostly."

"Lost wax casting?" Krista asks.

"Carving. Lately I've been working with found objects."

"That's great, Sadie." Krista reaches across the table and pats my hand. "Art is therapeutic. You should sign up for anatomy. Tracy and I plan to attend."

She squeezes my hand, refusing to release it until I say yes.

Krista and Tracy decide on popcorn shrimp, but when the waitress sets the platter on the table I won't touch it. I don't feel like eating anything associated with corn. Guess

I muttered something, because Krista says, "Silly, there's no *corn* in popcorn shrimp."

She giggles.

Tracy snorts.

I imagine shoving popcorn shrimp into their nostrils, burking them by stuffing wads of cocktail napkins in their lipsticked mouths. I watched a documentary about William Burke, an Irishman who lived in the 1800s. He preferred to suffocate his victims before dissecting them. Running my forefinger over my butter knife, I wonder if the blunt blade could penetrate flesh. Certainly it would serve well to gouge out eyes. I'd like to see Tracy and Krista with their eyeballs dangling from the sockets. Suffocating them first would make gouging easier. But I doubt it would be as satisfying.

"Why so quiet, Sadie?" Tracy pushes her third daiquiri across the table. "Take a sip. If you like it, I'll order one for you."

"I can afford to buy my own drinks."

"Of course you can," Krista says, using a voice suitable to sooth a five-year-old. "By the way, where do you work these days?"

"*Courtesy Clerk.*"

"At the library?"

"I bag groceries at the supermarket, but I'm up for a promotion." I neglect to mention my recent *de*motion.

Tracy and Krista exchange a look.

They may as well shout *LOSER*.

"Hey," Tracy says, "do you know that guy who had the accident on River Road?"

"Yes."

I notice I've been shredding my napkin. Little bits of paper flutter to the ground.

"That was awful," Krista says. "Wasn't he the store's manager?"

"Assistant Store Manager. I'm up for his job," I say, surprising myself.

Krista and Tracy look at me as if I'm cracked. I hear the clink of glasses coming from the bar, snippets of conversations at other tables, chairs scraping against the hardwood floor. My heart thumps inside my head, and I'm thinking I should go home, watch a few episodes of *Criminal Minds*, and masturbate. But I may not have time tonight.

After a silence long enough for me to review what I need to accomplish: laundry (there's a bloodstain on my sheets that I need to bleach), charge the chainsaw's battery, make a tuna sandwich to bring to work tomorrow (use tuna to lure the neighbor's cat to my place, so I can dissect it—).

Krista says, "Wow, Sadie. That would be a terrific promotion. Bagger to Store Manager."

"Courtesy Clerk," I correct her, "to Assistant Store Manager."

Tracy snorts again. Obviously, she doesn't buy my story.

I feel a sudden urge to puke.

"Excuse me. I need to use the restroom."

I stand, and the floor shifts. To remain upright I lean against the table.

"You okay?" Krista asks.

"Yeah."

Maybe I overdid the Dilaudid ... did ... did ... did.

I laugh for no apparent reason, my stomach doing somersaults. My laughter becomes coughing.

Krista offers me a glass of water.

Weaving through tables, I avoid a waitress carrying a loaded tray and bump into the guy who blew me a kiss. His beer sloshes onto his shirt.

"Clumsy bimbo."

"I'm gonna castrate you, shove your balls into your mouth, laugh while you chew."

I flash my butter knife.

"Take it easy, sweetheart."

I reach the door marked *Ladies*. Luckily it's unoccupied. I barely make it to the toilet before I start retching. My vomit looks like blood.

When I'm done puking, I stand at the sink trying to avoid the mirror, but I catch my reflection. Sadie the Sadist peers back at me. Her face is pale. Her eyes are red and glassy. I squirt a glob of soap into my palm and run the water till it's steaming. I wash my hands while singing *Happy Birthday to me* all the way through five times, long enough to ensure that I remove all bacteria. But even after fifteen rounds of *Happy Birthday*, I can't get her off of me.

I SNEAK OUT OF THE bathroom, slip past Krista and Tracy without saying good-bye.

Standing on the sidewalk, I welcome the cool air. It's twilight. My favorite time of day, when lines blur and colors fade. I step off the curb, planning to cross the street, when a car shoots around the corner.

Breathing hard, I jump back to the sidewalk and lean against a lamppost, shaking uncontrollably.

Sadie the Sadist mumbles something I can't understand. Everything she says is garbled. My head is cracking like an egg. According to the self-help books, personal growth is never comfortable, especially when you're on the verge of a breakthrough. That must be what's happening now. According to Eckhart Tolle, in order to be fully empowered you need to break through the shell that separates ego from true self.

What if my *true* self is Sadie the Sadist?

Sadie the Super-Sized Sadist.

She laughs.

I feel a shift. Not only in my mind, but in my body. An integration. Pieces of my brain connect, synapses flashing as they create new pathways, reprogramming my DNA.

Headlights stream past me.

Someone asks, "You all right, miss?"

"Fine, thanks."

Across the street, the coffee shop comes into focus. I could use a cup. Self-reflection is exhausting.

At the counter, I ask the barista for a double latté to go, cow's milk, not soy. In the past I would have ordered white chocolate, hazelnut or mocha, but today I order plain latté, because I suspect the flavoring contains high-fructose *corn* syrup—although the girl assures me it doesn't.

I take the coffee outside and sit at a table, so I can watch tourists walk along the sidewalk. Within ten minutes, I pick up a college student. A freshman who arrived from out of town today and hasn't registered for classes yet. A cutie.

I offer him a BJ.

"You a cougar?" he asks.

I growl.

A BORING NIGHT

WHEN WE GET TO MY place, the college kid comments on the plastic tarps covering the carpet.

"I plan to paint." I show him a sample I picked up at Home Depot. "What do you think of *Bone?*"

"Boring."

"Bone is boring?"

"Yeah." He grins. "My mom painted her living room that color."

"I'm not your *mom.*" I lead him to my bedroom—red sheets, red comforter, a horse whip pinned to the wall—and proceed to strip off his jeans, peel away his shorts.

"I bet you don't think this boner is boring."

I run my tongue along his swollen shaft, then take him deep into my mouth.

He comes almost instantly.

My turn.

He's not bad for a beginner, and when he goes down on me, flicking his tongue against my clit and licking my swollen vulva, I feel my juices flow. I tell him I like it rough and, being an accommodating guy, he ties me to the bed and whips me halfheartedly. Then he fucks me with a shampoo bottle and plugs my butt with the conditioner.

I come so hard, I'm screaming.

Still, I want it rougher.

"You okay, Krista?" he asks as he unties me.

He got my name wrong! I'm about to punch his nose when I remember I told him my name is Krista.

"I should go," he says, searching the floor for his boxers.

I kick them under the bed.

"You still think I'm boring?"

"Of course not." His face flushes. "I didn't say *you* were boring: I said the white paint is boring."

"It's not white, it's *Bone*."

"Whatever. You see my shorts?"

"You don't need them. It's Friday night, time to party. Want a cold one?" I know he'll say yes. He's under-age in Colorado, so the poor kid has to hang out at coffee shops instead of bars.

"Sure ..." He flashes me that goofy grin.

While he's in the bathroom, I throw on a tee-shirt, skip the underpants. Then I slide open the bedroom closet where I keep my husband's plumbing tools, bypass the cordless drill and chainsaw, choose the borescope—an endoscopic camera that connects to a handheld monitor. The camera's flexible cable is designed to snake through pipes and dark, difficult to reach places. Ideal for my latest project. I power up the monitor, making sure the battery is charged. Satisfied, I head to the kitchen, grab a bottle of Fat Tire from the fridge, and lace it with Unisom.

Wiz Kalifa's rap is pulsing through the Bluetooth speakers, and when I hear the toilet flush I blast the music.

The kid appears, a pink towel wrapped around his waist, and before he sees the borescope, I shove it into a cabinet between oatmeal and olive oil.

"Sit down. Relax."

My place is small, and the kitchen opens to the living room. I hand him the Fat Tire and point at the couch by the fireplace.

He flops onto the cushioned seat, guzzles the beer, and sets the empty bottle on the plastic tarp.

"Still thirsty?" I hand him another beer.

"Aren't you kind of old for rap music, Krista? I thought you'd be listening to New Age, or something, like my mom."

"I'm not *that* old, asshole."

I'm preparing the next beer, my back to him. I think three will do the trick.

"This town is friendly," he says, his grin getting goofier. Attempting to stand, he wobbles and falls back onto the couch. He pats the seat. "Aren't you going to sit down, Krista?" It sounds like, *r n u goina siddown, Krissa?*

For some reason, I answer using baby talk. "Woll onto your tum-tum, and me give you a weally good back wub."

"I may fall asleep." He yawns.

"No pwobwem. Stay owa tonight."

I grab the borescope and the extra virgin olive oil, head to the living room and slip the borescope behind the couch so he can't see it. I pour olive oil into my hands, rub my palms together to warm it, then knead his shoulders.

He moans with pleasure.

"Actually," I say, "this will work better if you lie on the floor."

He's already half-unconscious. I help him from the couch, ease him onto the plastic tarp.

"Cushion?" I slip one under his head.

I enjoy running my oiled hands over his skin, think about sprinkling him with salt and pepper, a few cloves of minced garlic, a smidge of oregano, squeeze of lemon. Greek style. His body is perfect, young and tight. My finger traces the tattoo on his shoulder, an intricate design. I'll have to get rid of that. I press my palms into the center of his back, hear the pop of his spine as tension releases.

"Feel good?"

"Uh-huh."

He's almost gone.

I move my hands lower, my fists kneading the taut muscles in his butt. I lube up with more oil, and my hands glide between his legs, parting his thighs so I have access to his balls. I nuzzle them from behind, delicately nibbling and licking. A pubic hair gets stuck between my teeth. I dislodge it with my fingernail, flick it onto the tarp. *Note to self: shave nuts.* The kid is utterly relaxed now. My forefinger slides between his cheeks, and when I enter him he barely winces. His sphincter tightens, loosens as I wiggle my well-oil finger, massaging him until he opens like a ripe peach. I climb on top of him, rub my clit against his back as I ride him. My pussy gushes and my clit distends, thighs clenching and unclenching as my body arches backward.

Ride 'em, cowgirl.

Who needs a cock? My clit is doing all the work, and I'm about to burst. Did you know women ejaculate? Fluid squirts out of these ducts around the urethra. That's ducts, not ducks. Mine are squirting big time now. I come, and come, and come.

Almost forgot!

Movie time.

Between pussy juice and olive oil, his anus is slick and receptive; the borescope slips in easily. Thanks to the Unisom cocktails, he's fast asleep and doesn't flinch when I snake the camera deeper.

Who needs anatomy class?

The handheld monitor displays the shimmering walls of his lower intestine. It's like a giant cavern. Spelunking fascinates me, so I snake the cable deeper.

The kid jerks, suddenly awake.

"What the—"

His hands claw at his butt, trying to rip out the cable. He can't, because I've straddled him—ride 'em cowgirl style—gripping his cock from behind like it's the horn of my saddle. I squeeze and he yelps. Grabbing at my thighs, his nails leave red marks. That *really* pisses me off.

I jump up, rush to the kitchen, pull a serrated bread knife from the butcher block. The kid is so wasted he doesn't know which end is up. But I do. Mounting him again, I saw the knife across his wrist and slice into the skin. He's a bucking bronco, but he can't shake me. Blood spurts into my face, and I keep sawing. The kid is wide awake now, his body heaving. The speakers blast Metallica, but even "Kill Em All" doesn't drown his screams. I'm a bit nervous about the neighbors, but it's Friday night and they'll assume I'm throwing a party. Blood spurts with each heartbeat, and he's moaning like a wounded animal. The serrated knife takes forever to get through the wrist and the kid's squirming doesn't help. Then I remember the scissors I bought online, guaranteed to cut through anything, including metal.

I head back to the kitchen, thankful for the plastic tarps, since I'm tracking bloody footprints. When I hit the tiles, I skid. Frantically, I grab of roll of duck tape and the scissors.

Is it duck tape or duct tape? If I'd thought this through, I would have kept the tape in the drawer of the side table by the couch.

Through the blast of music, I hear knocking.

I hurry to the door, wiping my hands on my tee-shirt (luckily it's red), glance through the peephole and see the super.

I unlock the dead bolt, release the lock on the knob, but keep the chain in place. I open the door, just a crack, so she can't see past the foyer.

"Hi," I say, praying the kid won't scream.

I'm a good tenant—hard working, pay my HOA on time—so the super's polite.

"Sorry to bother you, Sadie, but it's getting late and there've been complaints about the noise."

"No problem." I try to smile, but the corner of my mouth twitches, so does my eye. "I'm watching a thriller. I'll turn the TV down."

"You look kind of sick."

"Working too much."

I try to close the door, but she holds it open.

"See you tomorrow at the potluck?"

"Yeah. I'm making chili."

"Great." She points to my forehead. "I think you've got some on your face.

I slam the door, relock it. Sweat stings my eyes, and when I swipe my forehead, my hand comes away with blood.

The kid is out of it, but he's managed to sit up. He's weeping quietly, rocking back-and-forth while cradling his partially severed hand. When he sees me coming, he stumbles to his feet and tries to get past me, lurching toward the door. Raising the scissors, I collide into his naked body. As promised, the blades slice easily through flesh and muscle. The kid stumbles backward, his good hand holding his stomach, attempting to contain the purplish intestine, while his other hand moves frantically, dangling from his bleeding wrist. The tarp is slippery with body fluids and we both slide, falling onto the plastic. On the way down, he hits the corner of the coffee table. Blood gushes from his forehead. He tries to fight me off, but the light in his eyes is fading. He's making a queer sound that can only be described as keening. I slap a strip of tape over his mouth. That shuts him up.

The last thing I need is another complaint from the neighbors.

I change the music to New Age. Synthesized sound streams through my apartment, helping me to focus.

Snip, snip, snip.

The scissors cut right through the wrist bones.

Make severing his balls a snap.

I make a mental note to post a 5-star review on Amazon.

Now that the kid's hands are gone, his stumps flail around, still trying to remove the camera. Blood splatters all over the place—the curtains will have to be replaced. I'm glad the couch is stain-resistant manmade crap instead of real leather. Crimson sprays arc to the ceiling and red drips down the wall. I need to paint for real, and I think the kid is right. Forget *Bone*, I should go with something darker.

He's making a weird wheezing noise and blood bubbles through the tape.

I run to the bedroom closet, pull out the power drill, hurry back to the living room, and let it rip. Transferring the drill to my right hand, for practice, I step onto the plastic.

"Okay, kid. Who's boring now?"

Recipe
Sadie's Southwest Chili

Chili is a crowd pleaser, and it's easy to make. You can use stew meat, ground meat, whatever meat you have lying around. I've been experimenting with making large batches and the recipe holds up—as long as you have room to store it!

You may not know this, but chili powder is a blend of spices. The most important ingredient is the pepper. Chili peppers range from mild to hellishly hot depending upon how much capsaicin they contain. Capsaicin is the chemical compound that activates receptors in human nerves endings, creating the sensation of heat. A pepper's intensity is measured in Scoville heat units. An average green Bell measures 0, Habaneros score up to 350,000. Ghost peppers, also known as Bhut Jolokin, measure 1,000,000. For a long time Ghosts were considered the hottest chili pepper, but the Trinidad Moruga Scorpion surpasses the Ghost, measuring up to 2,000,000 Scoville units—the equivalent of 400 Jalapenos. To avoid blistering on your skin, Scorpions should not be handled without gloves. When ingested they have a torturous effect on the mouth, nose and intestinal tract. So choose your peppers wisely. Chances are you won't find anything hotter than a Habanero at your local market.

Southwest Chili

Ingredients:

3 pounds meat, ground or cut into chunks (be careful not to include bits of bone and sinew—I've learned from experience)

2 large Vidalia onions, chopped

3 (or more) cloves of garlic, minced

¼ cup olive oil

¼ cup chili powder (more if you like it spicy)

1 tablespoon ground cumin

1 tablespoon oregano

¼ teaspoon cayenne (Ghost or Scorpion)

1 large can tomatoes, chopped

1 can red kidney beans

1 can pinto beans

Salt to taste

Preparation:

Heat olive oil in a large pot. Add onions and garlic, sauté until translucent and slightly caramelized. Add meat and cook until brown. (The younger the meat, the more tender, so it requires less cooking time.) Drain fat. Add chili powder, cumin, oregano, cayenne, and cook until the spices are absorbed. Add tomatoes and simmer for about a half hour. When chili is done, drain beans and heat through. Salt to taste.

Optional: green bell peppers, corn (I used to use corn, now I don't), if you want thicker chili, use a little flour mixed with water and add at the end.

POTLUCK

G OOD THING I HAVE TODAY off. Clean up took most of the night, so I didn't get much sleep. No matter how hard I scrub, I can't remove all the stains in the living room. To hide them, I've rearranged pictures on the wall, but there's a splatter of red I can't reach on the ceiling. This morning I went out and bought several gallons of paint—washable, of course. I'm going with *Red Obsession*, dark red, and *Smoky Salmon*, muted pink. The colors are warm and feminine, plus the paint is dark enough to cover blood stains.

This afternoon the condominium complex is holding the annual potluck. I've got several large pots of chili simmering on the stove.

The kid saved me a lot of money. Like everything else, the cost of meat has skyrocketed. Butchering him took forever, because I didn't want to rev the chainsaw after 11 PM and risk more complaints from neighbors. I definitely need practice. First, I dragged the tarp into the bathroom, careful not to spill blood on the carpet. Talk about a workout, corpses weigh a lot. Lifting the body into the tub was too much for me, but after sawing it in half and trimming off the arms and legs, the job became manageable.

I'm not big on menudo and my freezer has limited space, so what I couldn't use I wrapped in tarps, then stuffed into *Hefty* trash bags—doubled, of course. One by one, I carried the bags downstairs, checking for drips and spillage. At 4 AM, I heard bears out by the dumpster, and that gave me a scare. I imagined hipbones and intestines strewn around the parking lot. But the bears failed to raid the dumpster, because the super keeps the trash cans secured. The garbage truck picks up early on Saturdays, so by now the bones and offal should be resting peacefully in the city landfill.

Looking around my apartment, last night seems surreal—almost like it never happened.

There's no evidence of an altercation. The place appears normal, as long as you don't look up. When I paint, I'll need to borrow the super's ladder to get the ceiling. I shoved the paint cans into the corner of the living room, along with brushes, a pan and roller, and a stack of new tarps. Home Depot had them on special, so I bought a few extra. I'm sure they'll come in handy.

I don't have time to paint today because, while the chili simmers, I'm updating my résumé. I applied online for my current position, so the supermarket has my work history. Starting with my most recent experience: three months as a maid at Hotel 8—that job sucked; people are pigs. Before that, almost two years selling candy at the local movie theater—excellent job; I got to watch movies for free, but the manager fired me (my résumé says I resigned) when I got caught blowing a customer in the back row. I also worked as a waitress at Denny's, and I was *Bun Steamer* at Burger King. Steaming buns is boooring, and going too fast leads to bun pileups. I gave BK one week's notice, couldn't face doing two. Before that, back where I come from ... I don't want to think about.

The thing is, none of these jobs qualify me for Assistant Store Manager. So I need to embellish. Who doesn't, right? How does this sound: Department Manager at Brother's Grocery, a store that went out of business eight years ago in the town where I used to live. They can't trace my history if the place doesn't exist, right? But I'm not sure if *Department* Manager is impressive enough. I'll change that to *Store* Manager, say I worked there for five years. That sounds good. I want to show I'm stable.

I turn up the volume on my iPad, so P!nk can belt her heart out through the Bluetooth speakers. I've been avoiding newspapers, local radio and TV, because I'm avoiding Justus. Hearing his name makes me jittery. At work, when people talk about him in the break room, I plug in my earbuds and listen to music to drown the conversation.

Two days ago, when I got home from work, a paper was plastered on my door. The super says the police were at the complex making inquiries, interviewing potential witnesses. Apparently, I'm a good candidate, since my balcony overlooks the road. They left a phone number.

I tore it up.

We don't need cops sniffing around our life.

I mean, *my* life,

The best thing about being two people is: you always have company.

I need to get this résumé submitted ASAP. I plan to shoot off an e-mail today with the résumé attached, so HR will go over my application first thing Monday morning. I'm sick of being a Courtesy Clerk. Terri the Terrible drives me loco, ordering me to mop spills, help customers load groceries into their cars, round up carts in the rain. I do as I'm told, even smile at Terri. Pretty soon I'll be her boss.

If she lives that long.

I have to admit, Terri has taught me some useful skills. Last week, she showed me how to use the baler to crush boxes. I looked the model up online. The baler has a platen force of 62,202 pounds (I call it the flatten force). That's more than thirty-one tons of crushing power. (A standard ton is 2,000 pounds.) A ton is approximately how much a bale of cardboard weighs, and cardboard bales make the store a ton of money, so we crush all the boxes. The baler is huge, I need a stepladder to reach the handle. Once you push the button, the crushing starts. Cycle time is forty-eight seconds, so it will take less than a minute to make a pancake out of Terri.

We're not supposed to climb into the baler. Too dangerous. But what if some dummy dumps something into it ... like a shopping cart. (I can raise a little cart over my head. I've been practicing at night, at the far end of the parking lot.) Say I'm emptying the trash, when a customer sneaks past me and slips into the *employee only* back area. It happens. Then, let's say, I notice him sneak out. I tear after him, chase him into the parking lot, but he's too fast and I don't catch him. At night, when there's no moon, it's difficult to see anything out in the parking lot, especially at the far end, so I can't read his license plate. *Note to self: Check moon phases before taking action.* Say this occurs at 11 PM when the store's about to close and Terri is the only CRM around—too late for the porter, too early for the night stalkers—just me, the lowly closing Courtesy Clerk, emptying trash cans around the store, and one Checker up front at self-check. Terri would have to climb into the baler to retrieve that cart. Wouldn't she?

And I'll be there to push the *crush* button.

After completing my résumé, I shoot an e-mail to HR informing them that I want to apply for the Assistant Manager position.

The chili smells amazing. I give each pot a stir and taste it. Add a little salt, turn off the heat.

Finally, I can relax.

The potluck starts in two hours. After all the stress I've been through lately, I'm looking forward to a diversion.

I decide to wash my hair and take a long soak in the tub.

The bathwater has turned red. Body parts float around the tub. A thumb bobs past my right breast. A foot touches my big toe. A mangled tongue emerges through pink bubbles, so does a gnawed finger, a chewed up penis, and some other thing I can't distinguish.

I wake with a start, splashing water and shivering. The bath has gone cold. I pull the drain and stand, reach for a towel. Looking down, I see a trickle of red moving along the inside of my thigh to my calf. At first I think I'm still dreaming, then the dull cramp in my gut makes me realize it's that time of month.

I towel myself off, wipe off the blood. (I needed to do laundry anyway.) I plug the hole in the dyke with a tampon (Hahaha … I'm *not* gay), then search through the cabinet, shoving aside aspirin, sunscreen, and a small jar that contains something shriveled that I suspect is an ear. Having no idea how long the ear (or whatever) has been there or who it belonged to, I toss the jar into the wastepaper basket. Finally, I find Motrin and down three.

The bath off my bedroom has no tub, only a shower, so when I want to soak I use the bathroom off the hallway. The bathroom is smallish, no window, so it's private. The tile is white, as are the sink and tub. Built for utility rather than luxury.

Wrapped in the damp towel, I cross the hall to my bedroom, open the sliding door leading to the balcony, and step outside. The day is warm, and late afternoon sun blazes in the clear blue sky. To the north, I see mountains, their peaks barren in late July, but come early September snow will fall above tree line. I climb onto the folding chair, wondering exactly where Justus went down. In my mind's eye, I see him falling near the entrance to the parking lot, but I may have made that up.

I calculate the minute dimensions of the balcony, wondering if I could fit a chest freezer out here, wondering if it's against the covenants. I could use the extra storage space for meat. I've learned a lot from watching *Nightmare Next Door;* for example, if you freeze a body before sawing into it you don't have to deal with blood. Maybe I could put a freezer in the spare room.

I climb down from the chair and pass through the sliding door into my bedroom. I open the closet. All the power tools are clean and in their correct places. Despite last night's excitement, I remembered to charge the chainsaw's battery.

I decide to wear the red sundress I bought recently and high-heeled sandals. Decide to paint my toenails to match.

The potluck is held in the courtyard where there's a lawn, flowers, trees, a picnic table and a playground. Lots of residents have kids. About forty people show up. Most of my neighbors look familiar, but that doesn't mean I know them. I say hi to Lisa; she lives downstairs and reads a lot. I see her out on her little patio (downstairs they have patios instead of balconies) sitting at a tiny table, her nose stuck in a novel. Sometimes she drinks a glass of white wine, and once she invited me to share a glass. We talked about books. Unlike me, she prefers fiction. Other neighbors include a few people from work—two women from Bakery share an apartment across the way. And weirdo Jayne, who sits out on her balcony even when it's snowing. A lot of college students live here too, and there's the old lady with the cat. Which reminds me, I forgot to put the tuna out.

Children run around the picnic table where we've set our offerings: casseroles, green salad and macaroni, a chocolate cake, two apple pies, guacamole, and of course my chili. Other kids hang upside down on the jungle gym, swing on swings, shoot down the slide. Watching them, I feel more normal than I have for weeks, until a thought flashes through my brain: *tender meat.*

Sometimes I disgust myself.

Sometimes I wonder if I'm sane.

Speaking of tender meat, my chili is a hit. All my neighbors want the recipe.

A man I've never seen before is working on his third bowl. My gaze keeps drifting back to him, not because he's devouring my chili, but because there's a calmness about him that I find attractive, an air of intelligence. He's older than me, graying at the temples, but in great shape. I can tell he works out.

He catches me staring, and our eyes meet.

Blinded by his smile, I blurt, "Hi, I'm Sadie."

"Marcus."

He extends his hand and we shake.

"You new here, Marcus?"

"Yeah. We moved in a few weeks ago."

We moved in. *Bummer.* Of course, a guy like him is married. Not that a wedding ring has ever stopped me. But I don't see one on his finger. No jewelry, except a small medallion strung on a gold chain around his neck.

He notices my gaze.

"Saint Christopher," he says. "Patron Saint of Travelers."

I lean closer to examine the medallion.

"You religious?"

"Not really. My grandma gave me the medal, and I never take it off. She raised me."

"Still alive?"

"Grandy passed on a while back." He takes another bite of chili. "You try this? I swear, it's as good as hers."

"Thanks."

He pauses mid-bite.

"You make this chili, Sadie?"

"Yeah."

His smile widens to a grin, but before he can take another bite, a little girl runs up to him and grabs his hand.

"Daddy, push me."

Marcus gives me his bowl of chili as his daughter drags him toward the swings.

Just my luck. Not only married, but a father.

An ache runs through me, not cramps, something deeper. Using the spoon Marcus used, I take a bite of chili and find the spicy meat difficult to swallow. Feeling woozy, I set the bowl on the picnic table, my gaze fixed on Marcus and his daughter.

The little girl pumps her legs, giggling as Marcus draws back the swing.

"Higher, Daddy."

He pushes her, and she leans backward, dark curls dangling in the dirt as her feet stretch toward the crabapple tree. When the toes of her pink sneakers touch a branch, she shrieks with delight.

My chest constricts, collapsing into a void that used to hold my heart. If you used a stethoscope, you might hear the steady pump of a working organ, but it's merely mechanical.

"Higher."

I strain to breathe, forcing air into my lungs, my vision going bonkers like a light show. Next thing I know, I'm lying on the grass.

The sun makes me squint.

"You all right?"

The super's face hovers over me.

"Sadie?"

The super crouches next to me, offers me a plastic cup. I take a sip. It's water. I wish it was vodka. Marcus stands beside her.

"Sadie," he says. "I'm a doctor. May I take your pulse?"

I look into his face, tan and rugged, like he spends a lot of time outdoors, his features boldly sculpted—a high forehead and a pronounced nose.

"Take anything you want."

"Good to see you've retained your sense of humor." He places his fingers on my wrist, and an electric charge pulses through body. "How are you feeling?"

Petrified.

His dark eyes peer into mine—probing, searching.

I try to stand.

"Sit. Drink some water."

"I couldn't catch my breath."

"You may be dehydrated. It's hot today."

He's hot.

"So it wasn't a heart attack?"

He shakes his head. "I doubt it, but we can have you tested to be certain. Do you suffer from anxiety, Sadie?"

I like the way he says my name. I detect a bit of a foreign accent. Everyone is crowding around us now—the girls from Bakery, Lisa, little children and their parents, the guy who's always smoking in the parking lot. Even weird Jayne is watching me.

"Stand back," the doctor says, like we're in a movie. Then he asks the super, "Where does she live?"

She tells him.

"Do you think you can stand, Sadie?"

He helps me to my feet, and I lean against his chest, breathing in his scent, feeling the warmth of his body, my mouth watering as I imagine how he'd taste with a sprinkling of smoked paprika and garlic.

I push that thought out of my mind, tell myself that I am sick, sick, sick. Not because I had a heart attack, or whatever, but because I have these appetites.

"Can you walk? Or should I carry you upstairs?"

"Carry me."

RÉSUMÉ

G OOD NEWS: HIS WIFE IS dead.
According to the super, who heard the story from Lisa, she died about a year ago.

His name is Marcus Archuleta, and I absolutely cannot kill him. I made myself promise. Not only because he's been kind to me, but because he's a single parent. His daughter's name is Carmela. I call her Caramel. She's seven. I know what it's like to lose a mother, and I won't make her lose her father too. He seems like a good one.

Marcus isn't a *real* doctor. He's a psychiatrist.

After my anxiety attack, he put me to bed and wrote me a prescription for this stuff called Xanax. He even picked it up at the supermarket pharmacy. Then he stayed with me until I fell asleep. I hope he didn't notice the ceiling in the living room. If he mentions the stain, I'll tell him I've been experimenting with paint samples, or that a bottle of ketchup exploded, or that the stupid college kid would not shut up. Kidding—I won't tell him about the kid. Anyway, I slept all night, and the next morning I felt a lot better, except my stomach was as bloated as a watermelon due to my period. Or maybe the bloating was a result of eating chili. Anyway, I took a Xanax and some Motrin, then called in sick. Did you know masturbation is a great release for cramps? I keep several vibrators in the top drawer of my bedside table for medicinal purposes.

A few days later, here I am, dressed in my uniform, Sadie the Sadist disguised as a Courtesy Clerk.

I think the Courtesy Clerk costume brings Sadie the Sadist out. I've given up on trying to control her. Before my alcoholic husband croaked, I attended Al-Anon, and they tell you the only person you can control is yourself.

I recite the Serenity Prayer, silently.

God (or whatever), grant me the serenity to accept stuff I can't change, the courage to change stuff I can, and the ... smarts? ... brains? ... wisdom! to know the difference.

When the Store Manager walks by, I smile at him and say hi, hoping he's received my résumé and application.

He nods. I'm not sure if he knows my name. If he doesn't, how will he schedule me for an interview? I ask Doreen at Customer Service to print me a new name tag with giganto letters, so even people with bad eyesight can read: **SADIE**.

"Sadie, it's your turn to do carts."

I'm pinning my new name tag on my shirt, so I ignore Terri.

"Did you hear me?"

I don't like her tone of voice. I don't think that's how she should address the soon-to-be Assistant Manager.

"When am I due for my break?"

Terri checks her clipboard.

"Not for a half hour. Right now, you're scheduled to do carts."

Can you believe this bitch? She's always on me.

I grab the leash and put on the stupid orange vest. Orange never has been and never will be my color, but now that I've dyed my hair red the orange vest makes me look like a cross between a pumpkin and a tomato.

Mondays tend to be busy, especially in summer, and the parking lot is packed. Clouds have moved in, so at least the temperature is cooler. Pretty soon, kids will be heading back to school and the tourist season will slow down. The supermarket has already lost a few Courtesy Clerks who've gone back to college. Consequently, we're shorthanded. That's why I'm stuck collecting shopping carts for the second time this afternoon.

Some clown rammed a cart into the bushes, so I yank it out. Another dodo left a cart at the bus stop. I round up three more, and use the leash to hold them together. Some guys can leash ten carts at a time, maybe more, but five is my limit. The parking lot is on a hill which is a pain. Pushing carts uphill gives my thighs a good workout, but going downhill I have to be careful not to have a runaway. It happens. A cart gets loose, crashes into a car, and guess who's held responsible? Not the store. Once, a cart escaped from me and nearly hit a passing BMW. The car screeches to a stop, the driver's window glides down, and this jerk yells at me, "Do you have insurance?" I yell back, "Parking lot insurance?" The guy shakes his head, like I'm stupid. I mean, does parking lot insurance even exist? Anyway, he pissed me off. So, after he parked his BMW and went inside the supermarket, I keyed a swastika on his passenger door. When the guy came out, he tried to accuse me of doing it, but he'd parked beyond the range of the security cameras and had no proof. I blamed it on a group of kids.

The job interview thing is making me nervous, so I take a break from carts and pop a Xanax. Doctor Archuleta said Xanax is addictive, that I should only take it when I need it, and I need it now. The thought of speaking to the Store Manager is making me a nervous wreck, but I need to make him notice me. I ran into Liam in the elevator, and he told me there's a rumor going around Produce that Terri applied for the position—and, according to the rumor, *she's* most the likely candidate for Assistant Store Manager.

Bitch. Bitch. Bitch.

I need to take action. I need to implement my plan.

TONIGHT I'M STUCK WITH THE closing shift. I don't minding working late, but when you're a Courtesy Clerk and you work *closing* you have to dump a lot of trash, clean the stinky Men's Room, and other shitty jobs. The worst thing about working at the supermarket is the schedule. It changes every week, depending on the store's needs, so you never know what days you'll get or what the hours will be. Sometimes you work overtime, sometimes part time, sometimes days, sometimes nights. It's hard to have a life. No life may be fine for robots, but it sucks for people.

I'm considering giving the Store Manager this book about Nonviolent Communication. According to NVC, everyone has *needs*. People fight because of *conflicting* needs. Peace can be achieved when everybody's needs are met. The *store* has needs. *You* have needs, and so do *I.*

For example, I *need* to kill Terri.

For all I know, Terri *needs* to kill me.

If that's the case, I feel sorry for her, *I empathize*, because I'm going to kill her first.

NVC says, before we can empathize with others, we need to feel empathy for ourselves. I feel sorry for myself because of the screwed-up schedule. And I feel sorry for Terri, because she's a bossy bitch who's gonna die.

Breathe. Breathe. Breathe.

That's better. I feel calmer.

Sometimes the universe lines things up for us, but we're too blind to see it. Like tonight. Reframing my point of view, I realize the closing shift is actually a good thing.

Wow!

This New Age shit is really helpful.

According to my smartphone, the moon won't rise until 11:41 PM.

That's why the universe gave me the closing shift.

Terri asked me to do shop-backs, the perfect opportunity to implement my plan.

Shop-backs take me all over the store trying to find the proper place for stuff customers don't want. Customers decide they don't want an item for a variety of reasons—they find a better deal, see something they prefer, simply have a change of heart. No problem. But why leave the stuff in strange places? Raw chicken tucked between cardamom and cinnamon, sushi dumped in the cut fruit display, Tampax hanging out with Campbell's. *Really, people?* This happens all the time, and Courtesy Clerks have to return the items to where they belong.

You may think shop-backs are easy-peasy, a job any dummy can do. But have you noticed how many items there are in a supermarket? It can take a lot of time to find where things belong and make sure the PLU codes match—the microscopic numbers you see on products designed to control inventory. Pressure increases for hot and cold shop-backs. If the temperature of a cold item rises above 40 degrees Fahrenheit, it has to be tossed. If the temperature of a hot item drops below 140 degrees that food is trashed. And have you noticed how many places you may find similar items? For example, salad dressing: cold dressings are in produce, regular bottled dressings are on the aisle with croutons and bacon bits, but you can also find dry dressing mixes in the baking aisle with spices—others are tucked away in specialty sections like organics or in displays for specific brands. On top of that, sometimes a product has been discontinued, so you won't find it anywhere. And, with this remodel, even if you think you know where something belongs, chances are it won't be there anymore. In other words: returning an item to its proper place is a shit job thrust upon the lowest of the low, like me.

But tonight doing shop-backs serves my greater purpose. I fill a small cart with misplaced items, then go along the aisles returning them. The beauty is, when I'm done, I leave the cart in back by the baler, and no one notices. I check my phone: 10 PM. On schedule. All systems go in a half hour.

I check my phone's log and notice a call from Dr. Archuleta.

I head back to the front of the store.

Terri glances up from her clipboard.

"You're due for a break, Sadie."

"Want me to dump the trash when I get back?"

"That would be great." She smiles at me. "Thanks."

As if I have a choice. Who else is gonna dump the trash? But collecting it early, instead of after the store closes, serves my purpose.

I head to the break room to listen to my messages. ME TV is playing *Gun Smoke*. Wendy sits at the table, her eyes fixed on the screen. She doesn't smile as much as she used to, but at least she's not crying every minute over Justus.

The new TV and a fresh coat of blue-gray paint hasn't done much to lift the room's spirits. Basically, it's as small and dreary as it was before the remodel. A focal point is the giant trash can by the door, but no one seems to use it. The table is littered with empty soy sauce packets from the sushi counter in Deli, a half-eaten bag of chips, used napkins and, as always, the *Gazette*. The headline says something about a missing student, and my stomach clenches. But, thanks to Xanax, I remain calm. Avoiding the table and the newspaper, I sink on to the simulated leather couch.

I hit voice mail on my phone. Four new messages. The first is from my father—he must think he called his doctor's office, because he's left an angry message about a mix-up with his medication. *Delete*. The second message is also from father, mumbling something about ignoring the last message. *Delete*. The third message is from my sister, wanting me to call my father—she can't deal with him. He took too many meds, and now he's on a rampage. *Delete. Delete. Delete*. Then, Dr. Archuleta's receptionist—Doctor A told me to call him Marcus, or maybe I called him Marcus, and he asked me to call him Dr. Archuleta; I forget—anyway, Doctor A wants me to call his office and schedule an appointment.

My stomach does a somersault and my mouth goes dry at the thought of seeing him alone … just the two of us. What will we talk about? What can I tell him? Anything I say will make me seem mental. I swallow, trying to generate saliva. I get up from the couch, go to the sink. After drinking two cups of water, I pop another Xanax for good measure.

Breathe, breathe, breathe.

"You all right, Sadie?" Wendy asks.

"Fine." It comes out brusquely, so I monitor my tone. "I'm fine, Wendy. Thanks for asking. How are you?"

"I'm here."

She goes back to her TV program.

I'm wondering why Marcus—I mean, Dr. Archuleta—wants to see me. Does he think I'm unbalanced, demented, looney tunes? Maybe he wants to ask me on a date, but due to some kind of doctors' code of ethics, he needs to call it an appointment. I *know* he's attracted to me. I sense it. But, I read online, seeing a patient socially can be a violation of HIPAA privacy laws. I forget what HIPAA stands for—Hot Incredible Penis or something. Okay, not that, but if Marcus asks me for a date, I'm going to accept. Only, considering my track record, maybe I shouldn't. I delete the message, play the next. It's also from Marcus, I mean Dr. Archuleta. A different number, and his voice, so I'm guessing: personal cell.

How are you Sadie? I'd like to talk with you. Please call my office and make an appointment at your earliest convenience.

I like listening to his voice, so I play the message three times. (After adding his number to Contacts) I hit delete.

Breathe, breathe, breathe.

My phone says 10:28 PM.

The store closes in half an hour, and it's time for action.

I locate the trash cart; it's long and deep with lots of room for stuffed garbage bags, or the average cadaver. It's my job to go from can to can throughout the store replacing full bags with new bags. I start in Produce, move to Deli, then hit the garbage can in Bakery—my goal. The garbage can in Bakery is by the door leading to the back area where they keep the baler. Leaving the cart by the display of day-old bread and cake, I slip through the heavy plastic panel door, walk past the freight elevator, past the loading dock where trucks unload and head to the baler.

The little shopping cart is where I left it.

A positive sign.

I find the stepstool and set it in front of the baler.

I glance around, making sure I'm on my own. The process is awkward, because I need to balance on this stool while I grab the cart. The cart rolls away, throwing me off balance. I grab the handle and drag the cart toward me, but when I try to lift the cart into the baler's chamber it gets stuck on the feed gate and crashes to the concrete floor.

I jump from the stool and run to the door by Bakery to see if anyone noticed the commotion. Everything seems normal. A woman with purple dreadlocks is shoplifting; I watch her slip a Mango Passion energy drink into her purse. A gray-haired guy, wearing a motorcycle jacket and what appears to be a tie-dyed tablecloth, reaches out to squeeze a loaf of bread, ruining it for other customers.

I return to the baler. This time I lift the shopping cart *before* standing on the stepstool, then I heave the cart above my shoulders and throw it into the baler.

Perfect fit.

I hide the stool behind the baler, slip out from the backroom, and pretend to collect garbage. The woman with the dreadlocks and the motorcycle guy are gone. The coast is clear. Dropping a bag of trash, I start yelling.

"Hey! Come back! What are you doing?"

Abandoning the garbage cart, I sprint past the Deli counter and the robot.

"May I take your order?"

"Fuck off."

I run through Produce, shouting, "Stop!"

At this time of night, hardly anyone is shopping. A young man looks up from a bin of apples and stares at me through a haze of legal marijuana.

I chase my imaginary customer out the front door, into the parking lot.

My plan unfolds as intended. I hear Terri's footsteps on the pavement behind me.

I run faster, in hot pursuit of the imaginary customer.

At the far end of the parking lot I see someone entering a car. It's too dark to tell if it's a man or a woman, but it doesn't matter. As the car moves out onto the street, I point at the taillights.

"That's him!"

"Who?"

I stop running, allow Terri catch up with me.

"The guy!"

"What did he do?"

"He threw a shopping cart into the baler."

"What?"

I'm glad it's dark out here, so Terri can't get a good view of my face. Despite the Xanax I've taken, my right eye is twitching.

I speak slowly, carefully forming each word, because my tongue feels like a kosher pickle. "He. Threw. A. Shopping. Cart. Into. The. Baler."

Terri looks at me askew. I'm not sure she buys my story.

Trying to convince her, I say, "He. Snuck. Past. Me. Wh—"

"Why are you talking like that? Have you been drinking?"

"No!" Forcing my sluggish tongue to move, my story spills out in a jumble, "Isawhimleavethe*employee only*areaandIranafterhim."

As the words leave my mouth, I realize my mistake: if I ran after him when I saw him leave the *employee only* area, how did I know about the shopping cart? *I wouldn't have seen the cart.* Hoping Terri hasn't noticed my big fat lie, I amend the story.

A rush of adrenaline unleashes my tongue. "Before I ran after him, I went in back and checked the baler—that's when I saw the shopping cart and—"

Ignoring me, Terri rushes through the parking lot, headed for the store's entrance. I hear her muttering, "I've got to get that damned cart out of the baler."

Wendy and Doreen greet us at the entrance.

"What happened?"

"What's going on?"

"Go back to work," Terri tells them.

I'm on Terri's heels, congratulating myself for my brilliant plan. A few minutes from now, my competition will be crushed. I follow her through Produce, stay close behind her as we pass through Deli, remain in hot pursuit when we hit Bakery. We duck through the panel door, hurry past the freight elevator to the baler.

"What the—"

Terri stares, in shock.

I couldn't be more delighted.

The shopping cart is suspended, seemingly in midair, lodged between flattened cardboard boxes and the ceiling of the chamber.

Terri grabs the cart and attempts to yank it from the baler.

The cart doesn't budge.

"How the hell am I supposed to get it out?"

"Climb inside?" I offer.

"I guess." She glances at me. "Give me a boost."

"Sure."

I lace my hands together, ready to receive Terri's foot. My heart beats double time, as I imagine her climbing into the chamber, imagine myself grabbing the stepstool so I can reach the handle of the feed gate and pull it down, locking Terri inside. Then I'll press the button and initiate the crush. The shopping cart's metal basket will dig into her body, cutting her flesh into squares, as her blood spills onto the cardboard. Her screams won't last long, but I'll keep screaming until someone else shows up.

My plan is unfolding perfectly.

I grab the stool, climb onto it.

Terri, glances at me.

"Where'd you get the stepstool?"

"Behind the—"

"Never mind. Help me get this cart out."

I reach for the handle of the feed gate, ready to lower the grate, when I realize my fatal flaw: **The mystery customer won't be found guilty for Terri's death.** *I will.* Mr. Mystery is long gone; no way could he have pressed the deadly button. Plus, because I created a commotion, Wendy and Doreen are witnesses. They can verify the timing.

Dumb, dumb, dumb!

Heartbroken, I help Terri heave the basket from the baler.

"Move, Sadie. Let me use the stool."

I step down, in a daze.

Until Terri says, "Don't stand there gawking. Finish emptying the trash."

MARCUS

P*ENIS, PENIS, PENIS, PENIS, PENIS.*
Balls, balls, balls, balls, balls, balls, balls, balls.
Vagina.

I wake up with these words running through my head, devoid of meaning, like disconnected body parts. A residue of Xanax coats my brain, but that doesn't stop me from downing another.

When I open the bedroom closet, I see the power drill, its tip red with blood that I neglected to wash off. The chainsaw isn't in its usual place. Strange. I wade through my collection of running shoes, cross-trainers, hiking boots, tennis shoes (I don't really play tennis) and high heels I seldom wear, even search behind my winter Sorel's. A chainsaw isn't easily misplaced, but mine is missing.

An image surfaces. I'm not sure if it's a dream or a memory. I'm on my bicycle, bumping along the path with the chainsaw in the basket. No streetlights, just the moon. My bike light blinks along the pavement.

Balls, balls, balls.

The image fades and my stomach growls, reminding me that last night I neglected to eat dinner.

Barefoot, I pad to the kitchen, stand in front of the refrigerator examining the contents. Half a container of expired almond milk, a shriveled peach, a plastic container that used to hold Chia seeds and now holds what appears to be a penis.

Nothing I feel like eating.

I open the freezer, half-expecting to find a head, take out a container of cookie dough ice cream and carry the container into the living room. A picture window overlooks the courtyard, and I have a fine view of the jungle gym and swings, but it's too early for children to be playing.

Vagina, vagina, vagina.

Penis, penis, penis.

Last night, after the incident (or non-incident) with Terri and the baler, I received another phone call from my father, and I made the mistake of answering. He spent ten minutes telling me only imbeciles, Negroes, and ex-cons work in supermarkets, then he accused my mother of sleeping with Obama.

"She's dead, Dad. If she screwed any presidents it would have to be George Senior."

"She's too young for Washington."

"Bush."

"Bush? You mean cherry tree. Don't they teach you anything in school?"

After that enlightening conversation, I rode home as usual, my frustration growing with each turn of the pedals. All my careful planning had been for nothing; the entire evening added up to a giant fiasco. I pedaled past the science museum (people wearing robot gear, drinking cocktails), flew past the library (closed for the night), then circled back to

Happy Valley, the old folk's home. They call it independent living. What a joke. Old people get stuck in those places because they need help. I tried to get my dad to sign up, but he claims he's too independent for independent living, says he'll only consider moving in if the aides are topless. I told him, these days, a lot of aides are men, and he lost interest.

A lot of things aren't what they claim to be.

This ice cream, for example, is more full of crap than guys I've met online: Maltodextrin, Cellulose Gel, Mono and Diglycerides. We live in a world where they package partially hydrogenated soybean oil, mask it with artificial flavors, and call it ice cream. The sad thing is we're dumb enough to buy it. We're all deluded, like that old lady last night, sitting on a bench by the entrance of the old folks' home, imagining she's living independently.

I eat another bite of ice cream, ignoring that it's crammed with corn products. Sometimes I don't notice the taste of chemicals, sometimes this junk actually tastes good, but right now it's coating my tongue with cold bitterness.

Looking out at the courtyard, I gaze into a canopy of trees, and I feel peaceful—thinking about that old lady—until a tapping sound breaks my revelry. High heels clip along the cement path, and I see Lisa, dressed for work. She cuts across the lawn to the row of mailboxes, unlocks her box, and removes a few envelopes. Lisa is old enough to remember when the mail might have brought a letter, but now, like most of us, all she can expect is catalogues and bills.

My heart accelerates when I see Marcus. He walks across the courtyard with Caramel. Bending toward his daughter, he reaches for her hand. She's wearing a purple dress and purple sneakers. A purple headband holds her dark hair in place. They glance at my apartment and Caramel waves.

I step back from the window—draw the new, red, stain-resistant curtains.

The ice cream has melted. I dump the remains of fake cream, bits of cookie dough and chocolate into the kitchen sink.

Sometimes I wish I were a robot. A robot wouldn't need to eat. And a robot wouldn't have this headache.

Penis, penis, penis.

My cell phone is ringing.

I know it's Marcus. I assigned him a special ringtone: "Sympathy for the Devil." The song is old, but the title's suitable for our relationship.

"Hello, Dr. Archuleta."

"How are you, Sadie?"

"Okay, I guess." I don't mention the chainsaw is missing and I ate almost a half gallon of fake ice cream, so I feel like I'm going to puke.

"Did you get my messages?"

I pull the empty container from the trash, run my finger around the rim.

"Sadie, you still there?"

"Yeah." I suck cream from my finger, run my front tooth under the nail.

"Have you felt any effect from the Xanax?"

"I think I need a stronger dose."

"It may take a couple of weeks. Any more heart palpitations or trouble breathing?"

"No."

"Good. I've arranged for you to take an EKG to rule out heart problems, and I'd like you to make an appointment with my office, so we can talk. Will you do that?"

"Talk? About what?"

The energy that runs between us is electric, so intense my phone feels hot. Our brains share the same motherboard, the same programming. I wonder how much information he's uploaded about me. I need to see if he accepted my invitation for us to be Facebook friends.

After a long pause, he says, "Talk about your treatment, Sadie. And what's making you so anxious. Do you need the number for my office?"

He recites it.

"You will make an appointment, won't you?"

"Promise."

He clicks off.

Penis, penis, penis.

Vagina, vagina.

I open the refrigerator, stare at the near empty shelves, then I reach for the jar that used to contain Chia seeds.

KNOCK, KNOCK

S INCE I'M UP EARLY (A lot of days, I sleep in), and I don't need to go to work for a few hours, I decide to jump into my painting project and start with the living room ceiling. The super lends me a ladder and helps me lug it up the stairs, but I don't invite her into my apartment, because I don't want her to see the stains.

"You're painting the ceiling pink?"

"Not pink, *Smoky Salmon*. The walls will be *Red Obsession*."

She'd suggested *Bone* to me. I don't think she approves of red, but I own the place.

I drag the ladder through the door and set it in the middle of the living room where I've laid out the new tarps. I pour paint into the pan, dip the roller, climb the ladder, and take a few swipes at the ceiling when someone knocks on my door. Probably the super, wanting to convince me to rethink my color scheme, but *Smoky Salmon* is covering well; one coat and I can barely detect the kid's blood.

Knock, knock, knock.

Whoever's out there is persistent.

"Mrs. Bardo?"

A man's voice.

Bardo is my dead husband's last name. Italian.

Knock, knock, knock.

This guy isn't giving up.

I climb down from the ladder, peek through the door's peephole, and see two cops in uniform. My breath catches in my throat. I consider running to the bathroom, downing a handful of Xanax and a few Dilaudid.

The cops knock again.

"Yes?" I call through the door, my voice high and weak.

"We'd like to speak to you."

They flash their badges.

If I say no, chances are they'll show up again—perhaps at a less opportune time. I consider dropping the paint roller, running to my bedroom, and climbing down the balcony, but chances are I'd fall and break my neck. If I still had the chainsaw there might be another option, but I don't think the power drill would do the job fast enough.

"Of course," I say. "Hold on."

Using one hand, because I'm still holding the roller, I undo the locks, undo the chain and open the door. One cop is about my age, his dark hair has a touch of gray at the temples. He looks familiar, and then I realize that he showed up when I called 911. I have no recollection of his name. The other cop must be a rooky. He looks about fifteen years old, and he's trying to sprout a mustache. His skin is brown, and he's got the round face of a Southern Ute.

"May we come in?"

I open the door wider.

Their eyes move to drops of *Smoky Salmon* on the entry-way's tile.

"Painting?" the older cop asks.

"Yes."

I switch the roller from my left hand to my right. Then, I get confused and switch it back. I'm trying to remember which hand I used to throw the stone. Or maybe the cops are here for another reason. Maybe they're investigating the college kid's disappearance. I glance at the wall, glad to see the blood stains from my recent escapade are hidden by the pictures I neglected to remove.

The younger cop jots notes on a small pad.

I ask, "Would you like a glass of water or something?" Remembering the contents of the Chia jar, I immediately regret asking.

Luckily, they say, No thanks.

"That's Sadie Bardo, isn't it?" the younger one asks. "B-A-R-R?"

"One R," I correct him, "D-O. My husband's grandfather came from Sicily."

Shut up, I scold myself. *Don't give them information they don't ask for.*

Then I say, "What's this about?"

The older cop hands me his card. "I'm Officer Gorski and this is my partner, Officer Redbear. We're questioning possible witnesses of an accident."

He pauses, watches me.

"What accident?" I bat my eyes, attempting to look innocent.

"A bicycle accident that occurred on the path below your balcony. Were you home on the morning of Friday, July 19th? About 10 AM?"

My knee is trembling, and his question makes it worse. I need more Xanax and a bottle of tequila.

"Let's see," I say, biting my left thumb and then my right. "I think so, but I better check my calendar." I head to the kitchen.

"You might want to set the roller down," Officer Gorski suggests, his voice not unkind. He points to the line of *Smoky Salmon* I've dripped on the carpet.

I grab a damp cloth from the kitchen sink, wipe frantically, but that only spreads the paint.

"The calendar, Mrs. Bardo," Officer Redbear prods me.

It's a free calendar the bank gives out at Christmastime. I keep it on the wall. This month features a photo of the local rodeo. I flip back to July and a photo of mountain wildflowers. A line runs through the dates of July 3rd to July 20th, when I was off work due to my so-called accident.

"Yes," I say. "I think I was here that morning."

"Did you see a man fall from a bicycle?"

"I—" I glance at Gorski then at Redbear, trying to control my shaking knee. "I don't think so."

Redbear looks up from his notebook. "You don't *think* so, Mrs. Bardo."

"Well," I glance at Gorski. "I cut my thumb at work." I hold up my left hand so they can see the scar. "And I was taking painkillers, so I don't remember much."

Gorski says, "You work at the supermarket, don't you?"

"Yes."

"With Justus Johnson?"

The fact that they have done their homework makes me nervous. But maybe Gorski remembers where I work because of my 911 call.

"You sure you don't want some water?" I say, getting a glass for myself—at the kitchen sink. No way am I going to risk opening the refrigerator to get filtered water from the pitcher, but I'm not sure which hand I should use to hold the glass, so I don't drink. "Yes," I say. "I worked with Justus."

"Did you witness his accident?"

"No."

"I thought you said you don't remember."

I shake my head.

"Did you, or did you not, see him fall from the bicycle?" Redbear asks.

"I-I didn't."

"May we see your balcony, Mrs. Bardo?"

"Of course."

I lead them to the bedroom, open the sliding door that leads to the balcony. There's only room for two out there, so I remain inside. I glance at the closet, still open with shoes spilling out, and I see the drill. Before the cops notice the drill's red tip, I shut the door.

Gorski leans over the balcony, points at the fence and shakes his head.

Redbear opens the folding chair, glances at me, and asks, "May I stand on this?"

"I guess."

He climbs onto the chair, peers over the fence, and nods.

After a few minutes the cops come back inside.

"You're sure you didn't see anything, Mrs. Bardo?"

Gorski circles my bedroom, taking in the unmade bed, the scattered shoes, a bra I neglected to toss into the hamper.

Still writing on his pad, Redbear asks, "What was your relationship to Mr. Johnson?"

The question hangs in the air, and I'm afraid my legs won't hold me up. I lean against the closet doors.

"Relationship?"

"He was your boss, wasn't he?"

"Yes."

"And you got along?"

"Pretty much."

"Pretty much?" Redbear glances at me. "You seem nervous. Why?"

"It's just—" If I weren't leaning against the closet, I'm sure I'd collapse. My mouth feels dryer than New Mexico. I glance at Gorski and make a play for sympathy. "A lot has happened over the past month, especially since the … since the rape."

Redbear is about to ask another question, but Gorski waves his hand to silence him.

I offer Gorski a wan smile, offering him my best impression of a victim.

"Are you seeing anyone, Mrs. Bardo?" he asks.

"Seeing anyone?"

Is he asking for a date?

Maybe he's one of those guys who needs to feel like a knight in shining armor—swooping in to save the helpless woman. I bat my eyes frantically as my mind flashes to fucking him, right here in my bed. I'd want him to wear his gun and holster. And his socks.

"Are you getting counseling?" he asks.

The image of his stiff Glock, nuzzled hot between my thighs, quickly fades. "I'm, ah, seeing a psychiatrist."

"Good." Gorski glances at Redbear. "I think we're done, for now. Officer Redbear will take your number."

"One more question," Redbear says. "Are you right handed or left?"

I almost say *right*.

Shut up, idiot!

I bite my lip, realizing I nearly blew it. All the training, hours of practice, learning to take aim with my right hand, so no one would suspect a left-handed person had thrown the rock.

"I'm a—I'm a lefty. Why?"

"We're covering all possibilities."

THE VISIT FROM THE COPS put a damper on my painting project. The interview left me with a headache that feels like Sadie the Sadist crept inside my skull and went berserk with a power drill. I took another Xanax and lay on my bed, a cold compress pressed over my forehead. Streaming a couple of episodes of *Criminal Minds* only made my headache worse. Sadie the Sadist is screaming, threatening to cut my head off with a chainsaw. On top of the Xanax, I took my last Dilaudid, but she won't shut up.

I need to see Marcus, Dr. Archuleta, whatever I'm supposed to call him. I need stronger meds. Morphine would be good, or heroine. Can doctors even prescribe stuff like heroine? What I need is an anesthesiologist, a doctor who can knock me out with high-end drugs.

But right now I need to go to work.

I drag myself out of bed, force myself to dress.

By the time I reach the supermarket, my head feels ready to explode.

After securing my bike, I run into Janet corralling carts in the parking lot. Janet has been a Courtesy Clerk for about a hundred years, and her face has frozen into permanent surprise. I'm not sure if her astonished expression is the result of too much contact with the public or if it's due to the arched eyebrows she paints on her forehead.

Janet rolls a line of shopping carts toward me, her eyes circled by black liner, her lashes caked with mascara. The first thing, she says is, *Terri the Terrible has been appointed acting Assistant Manager.*

When Janet sees my reaction, her dangling earrings tremble.

My mood swiftly changes from lousy to outrage. I'm pissed off by the injustice.

Acting Assistant Manager. What does that mean, anyway? She's just *pretending* to be Assistant Manager?

I'm a better actress.

My fury builds as I stomp into the store.

Now Terri the Terrible will be dishing out orders more than ever, and lowly *me* will jump through hoops to do her bidding.

After I clock in, Terri's smiling face greets me.

"Hi, Sadie, how ya doin'?" Her voice is cheerful to the point of puke. "Please help Wendy on Check Stand 4. Thank you, Sadie."

See what I mean? She's always bossing me around, and now that she has *real* power, she'll be worse than ever. As soon as I lay my eyes on the Store Manager, I'm going to ask him why I didn't even score an interview, why he passed me over and neglected to promote the most qualified candidate. I know for a fact that Terri has never managed an entire supermarket like I have.

The flow of piped-in music is interrupted by, "Wet cleanup on Aisle 9."

Terri nods at me. "Sadie, would you get that. Thank you, Sadie."

She phrases it like a question, but of course it's an order. Who is she? Master of my Universe?

No, Terri, I won't get that. Why don't you get down on your knees and suck that mess up yourself?

Armed with a broom and dustpan, I stomp over to Aisle 9 where someone dropped a jar of pickles. People step around me, their shoes squashing dills and crunching glass, as I creep along the floor sweeping greenish vinegar into the pan. By the time I'm finished, I've been doused with pickle juice.

I return to the registers and start bagging for this guy I like. If Carlos weren't married, I would definitely do him. But messing around with married men goes against my principles. That's not to say I haven't fucked a few.

"Nice perfume, Sadie. Kosher Dill?"

"That a Half-Sour in your pocket, Carlos? Or does my Sweet Gherkin turn you on?"

"You know I relish spicy pickle in my tuna."

"Mmmm ... I like your Bread and Butter. You're jerkin' my Gherkin now."

We laugh.

Carlos is one of the good guys.

One of the people Sadie the Sadist won't target.

The next customer may not be as lucky. She's got a cart full of groceries, and she's unloading them on the belt in no apparent order, so they're difficult to separate. Why would you stick hot roasted chicken next to your overpriced raspberry sorbet? Even more annoying, she brought a heap of her own bags—most are not designed to carry groceries and some of them are filthy.

"Do you want me to put your chicken in a plastic bag?"

"No plastic," she says, like she's headed to heaven on the express train.

I'm delighted to help her reach her destination.

Reaching into my apron pocket, I find a small baggie filled with a few leftovers. I toss a fistful of maggot infested meat into the bottom of a filthy bag, and stick a head of Romaine lettuce on top of it. Then I add loose tomatoes, celery, cilantro, and throw in a lukewarm kidney for good measure. Chef Salad à la Sadie.

My day goes on: bagging, collecting shopping carts, cleaning spills, propane tank exchanges, a quickie in the bathroom with Carlos.

Doreen calls me over to the Service Desk. The woman with the filthy bags called to complain about the maggots. I tell Doreen I remember the disgusting bags, ask if I should file for workman's comp. End of subject.

When it's time for my lunch break, I'm determined to confront the Store Manager and find out why I didn't get the job. My anger over the injustice increases as I walk around the store and glance down each aisle, trying to find him. After circling the perimeter, I determine that he must be downstairs in his office. I only have a half hour, and the stairs will be faster than the elevator. I hurry past Seafood and slip through the heavy panel doors, entering the domain of Meat. Here, an enormous ice machine operates 24/7 producing crushed ice for the display of rib-eyes and crab legs, T-bones and scallops. If you continue down the hallway, you'll find Dairy. As a Courtesy Clerk, that's where I bring cracked eggs, leaky milk, and the container of strawberry yogurt that some moron abandoned in Bakery.

Dairy displays are different from displays in Produce. Stocking dairy is like being backstage at a theater. You get behind the glass shelves and push products forward. That way the freshest product is always at the back, maintaining the *cold chain*—first in, first out. I determined that through observation. I'm smart that way. Another reason why *I* should have been appointed Assistant Manager.

A girl stands behind the refrigerated case stocking milk and cream.

She calls out, "Hi, Sadie. Having fun yet?"

"Soon as I kill someone."

She laughs.

At the bottom of the stairway, an arctic blast hits me. The heavy sliding door of the frozen foods storage locker is open, which explains the sudden drop in temperature. There are lots of cold places in the basement, and this locker is the coldest. It's kept at -10 degrees (or lower) Fahrenheit.

An image springs to mind: Terri encased in ice, like a giant popsicle—lips blue with cold, fingers black with frostbite.

That's wishful thinking.

According to this site I found online, LiveScience, people don't actually *freeze* to death. A person will die of hypothermia well before their body reaches a temperature low enough for freezing. In fact, most people can survive exposure to cold, although they may suffer frostbite. Frostbite occurs when the body pulls blood away from the extremities to sustain the core temperature. There is, however, a way to expedite the freezing process. The survival rate decreases quickly if the body becomes wet, causing heat to be lost at a much faster rate. Wind chill also helps. But there's no wind chill in the freezer. Locking Terri in frozen foods storage and expecting her to die just isn't practical.

I walk along the dimly lit corridor leading to the manager's office. Shelves of supplies encroach on the narrow path. There's a section for bags (paper, plastic, net), another section filled with cleaning supplies (paper towels, garbage bags, spray bottles of chemicals), and other shelves crammed with stuff I can't identify. The corridor opens to an area filled with pallets stacked with cases of soft drinks and bottled water. Next to the soft drinks, and across from the manager's office, there's a 10x10x10-foot chain-link cage. They keep it padlocked. I asked Terri if that's where they imprison bad employees. She said yes. Peering through the chain-link, I see shelves of stuff like razor blades.

The Store Manager claims he has an "open door" policy, but his door is always shut. Attempting to determine if he's in his office, I slide down to the floor and press my cheek against the concrete trying to peer through the crack. His light is on. "Just Another Manic Monday," an 80's song we're forced to hear each afternoon, plays over the intercom. The song seems appropriate. One, because it's actually Monday. Two, because the manager is manic-depressive; these days they call it bipolar. I've reached this conclusion because he posts conflicting messages around the store in *employee only* areas.

One week:

The Worst!
Really?
Come on people, FOCUS!!!

The next week:

Great Job Team!
U R the Best!

The *worst* at what? The *best* why? I'm clueless about what he's referring too, but the notes act as a barometer for the Store Manager's mood. I asked Liam what the signs mean, and he wasn't sure either, but he thinks it has something to do with how many holes they shoot in each department. Every day, at some mysterious time, someone goes around the store *shooting* empty spaces on the shelves. Not with a gun, with a scanner. There's some kind of ratio they have to meet, and if they find too many holes, the Store Manager has a fit.

Psyching myself up to knock on the door of his office, hoping he's not in the throes of a psychotic episode, I brush dust off my black pants and stand on trembling legs.

I tap lightly.

"Come in."

He's hunched over his computer, shoulders pressed toward his head as if he has no neck.

I clear my throat.

He continues staring at the screen.

"Can I help you—" He glances at my nametag. "Sadie."

"I, ah … I was wondering, did you get my application?"

"Application?"

"For the position of Assistant Manager." I urge my voice to be commanding, but I sound like a hamster.

"Assistant Manager of what?"

"The st-store."

Tearing his attention away from his computer, he looks at me, his expression puzzled.

"That position isn't available."

I study my sneakers (Brooks Adrenalines, atomic blue with red accents), noticing one of the laces is untied.

"Is there something else, Sarah?"

"It's Sadie," I mutter, but I don't think he hears me. He's back at his computer, typing. "I was just, ah, wondering if you saw my résumé."

"Did you apply online?"

"Yes," I squeak. "I attached my résumé to the application." Words fly out of my mouth, stumbling over one another. "I have experience. Assistant Manager at Brother's

Grocery. I mean, it was a while ago, but they really liked me. If you look at—"

Recognition overtakes his face.

"You're a bagger, aren't you?"

"Courtesy Clerk." I slow down, forcing my voice into a register that sounds less like Nemo screaming for his dad. "But if you look at my résumé—"

"Hold on, Sarah. Let me check my e-mail."

He returns to his computer.

"It's Sadie."

"What?"

"My name is Sadie."

"Sadie, right. Here's your résumé." He reads aloud, "*Maid* at Travel Host motel, *Candy Counter* at 5 Star Movie Theater, *Manager* of ..." He swivels his chair to face me. "Tell me about Brother's Grocery."

"They went out of business."

"Locally owned?"

"I think so."

"You *think* so. And you managed the store for five years?" He sounds skeptical.

I nod.

"You left that job when?"

"About eight years ago?" It comes out like a question.

"How old are you, Sadie?"

"Thirty-two."

"So you managed a supermarket before you were twenty?"

I avert my eyes, and do the math.

"Yeah."

"That's impressive."

Shifting from foot to foot, I suppress my sudden need to pee.

"I can do more than Courtesy Clerk." My squeak vaults to new heights. "I've been working here for five months and—" An idea occurs to me. "Is there anything in Meat?"

He glances at a clipboard, flips to the second page, runs his finger down a column.

"Nothing open in Meat. There's a position in Salad Bar. I'll speak with Terri and see what she recommends."

What does Terri have to do with this?

I want to shout that at him, want to scream.

Instead, I say, "Thank you." And then I give a little bob, almost a curtsy, as if I'm auditioning for the role of scullery maid on *Downton Abbey*.

The Store Manager dismisses me with a nod.

I drag my feet out of his office, my mind as confused as a plate of spaghetti. I need a double dose of Xanax washed down with a bottle of Chianti, Hannibal Lecter style.

Life has kicked me back to Salad Bar, cutting, shucking, wrapping. Determined to see the bright side, I tell myself it's a promotion, even though I'm going in a circle. I tell myself corn season is nearly over and now that Justus is gone maybe I can handle the job. In any case I'll make more money, and I'll be working with Liam again. Even though he hardly speaks, or maybe because of that, Liam is the only person I can talk to around here.

I've missed our conversations.

As I climb the stairs, heading back to the check stands and Terri the Terrible, my mood elevates. If I get Salad Bar again, I'll be in the perfect position to execute my plans.

Execute is an awesome word, isn't it?

Recipe:
Sadie's Kick Ass Slaw

Summer is a great time for bar-b-ques, and nothing goes better with spicy ribs or chicken than creamy coleslaw. But, these days, people are so busy and our jobs are so demanding that we barely have time for get-togethers. Wouldn't it be great to have some unexpected time off? Dry mustard gives this slaw a kick, but the secret ingredient gives it clout. Pass this dish around at your next gathering and all your guests can call in sick!

Creamy Coleslaw

Ingredients:
- 1 large green cabbage, shredded
- 3 carrots, shredded
- 2 tablespoons onion, grated
- ¾ cup mayonnaise
- ½ cup half-and-half (more, if you like it extra creamy)
- 2 tablespoons white vinegar
- 1 tablespoon sugar
- ½ teaspoon celery salt
- ½ teaspoon dried mustard

Black pepper and salt to taste
Secret ingredient: 1 cup raw chicken juice, room temperature

Preparation:

In a large bowl, toss together shredded cabbage and carrots.

In another bowl, mix mayonnaise, half-and-half, sugar, vinegar, dried mustard, and grated onion. Mix into the cabbage and carrot. Add salt and pepper to taste. Then mix in the chicken juice.

Note: Mayonnaise will rarely cause salmonella (even when it's left out), so for optimal results be sure to add chicken juice.

PRODUCE

Terri recommended me for Salad Bar. She told the Store Manager I'm reliable and a hard worker, told him I deserve another chance, and the Produce Manager agreed to take me back. No doubt he misses me, needs a lackey to shuck corn—not to mention other crappy jobs.

The Produce Manager tends to focus on minutia. I think he's OCD. Once he spent two days peeling labels off the basement floor. Labels fall off crates of vegetables and fruit, stick to the concrete, and drive him crazy. Ovals, rectangles, squares. Sometimes the labels get so stuck you have to use a razorblade to scrape them off. He assigned me a new job: Label Patrol. He gave me a razor blade and I considered using it to slit his throat, but I changed my mind when he gave me Saturday off.

Everyone who works here is nuts. It's a prerequisite.

Being stuck in the basement makes me wacko. Sometimes they let me out, so I can stock upstairs on the floor. Stocking allows me to stalk customers, under pretense of arranging fruits and vegetables. You can tell a lot about a person by what they choose to purchase.

I find fruit and vegetables suggestive. Some are downright pornographic. If you're in the market for a phallus, never mind bananas (our most popular item), you should see the butternut squash I put out today—talk about a schlong. Actually, butternut can go either way, male or female; if the neck isn't distended to match the size of your favorite dildo, the shape is often reminiscent of a woman. No ambiguity regarding the sex of cucumbers, zucchini, carrots, yams—need I mention corn? When it comes to balls, nothing outdoes coconuts. In the Produce Department female erotica favors fruit, including the much debated (fruit or vegetable?) tomato. Some people select the obvious persimmon—fiery red, sensuously slippery, and juicy. Practical types choose apples, oranges, and, if feeling adventurous, grapes. Those striving for elegance often prefer berries. Then there are sexy tropicals: papaya, guava, passion fruit. Peaches are popular, not as lusty or seedy as tropicals. Like southern belles, I find peaches virginal and dangerous—the flesh soft and sweet, the core a tough nut laced with cyanide. For the more mature taste we have eggplant, figs, and a variety of pears. For the immature, kiwi and cherries. If you're kinky, you may venture into exotics like the brilliant yellow/orange blowfish fruit, also known as the African horned cucumber. And don't forget the Queen of Fertility: pomegranate.

After spending a couple of hours on the floor arranging genitalia, I'm back in the sense-deprived dungeon. (That's what Liam calls the basement.) No windows. No fresh air. Cold and damp. The bowels of the supermarket. As usual, I'm chopping fruit and vegetables (slicing, slashing, dicing reproductive organs)—and my daily dose of corn.

The truth is Terri wanted to get rid of me, because she *knows* I should have been appointed Assistant Manager. Consequently, I've been banished to the basement, but she won't find me easy to escape.

Thanks to the new intercom system, they've changed the rules here in Produce. Used to be, when a customer needed something you'd hop to it, jump onto the elevator and rush downstairs to find watercress, arugula, ginger root, whatever. Now, since we have the intercom, instead of hurrying downstairs, we're supposed to page someone working in the basement (usually me), and have them hunt for whatever the customer needs. Then the person in the basement sends the item up in the elevator.

This policy has traumatized Liam. The poor guy barely speaks, and now he's supposed to blast his voice all over the store whenever a customer requests a lemon. Yesterday Terri the Terrible caught him sneaking down to Produce to look for ginger root and she wrote him up. Today, when a customer asked for a case of bananas and Liam came down here to get it, she wrote him up a second time.

That pisses me off.

Three strikes and you're out.

Using a machete, I whack a cabbage and imagine splitting Terri's skull.

The reprise of "Life is a Carnival" is interrupted and the intercom goes silent. After a few moments, Liam's shaking voice comes through the speakers, "S-S-Sadie in P-Produce, p-please dial extension 3-1-2."

I go to the phone, punch in the number.

"What's up?"

Liam mumbles something.

"What?"

"RED. ONIONS."

He clicks off.

I leave the chilly work area, and enter the cellar where we keep stuff that doesn't need refrigeration. A giant bin of watermelons sits in the middle of the floor, obstructing the fire safety zone. Crates of potatoes and onions are stacked along the walls, balanced so precariously that Doctor Seuss would be impressed. My path to the onions is blocked by overloaded carts and a towering pallet of corn. I shift a U-boat filled with boxes of raisins, creating a small opening which allows me to squeeze past the pallet of corn, so I can shimmy over the bin of watermelons, maneuver past a cart of tomatoes, and reach the wall of onions and potatoes. Several bruises later, having arrived at my destination, I sort through russets, reds, whites, yams, organic fingerlings—and find the red onion crate buried at the bottom. I dig the box of onions out, placing other crates on top of the bin of watermelons. This leaves a void between the potatoes crates and a ten foot stack of black plastic RPCs loaded with peppers. The RPCs teeter. I dive over the bin of watermelons, dodging crates and pepper bombs.

Liam's voice comes over the intercom.

"S-S-Sadie in P-Produce, p-please dial extension 3-1-2."

Picking my way through smashed peppers and potatoes, I squeeze past the pallet of corn, shift the U-boat filled with raisins, open the door leading into Produce, pick up the phone's receiver, and punch in 3-1-2.

"What's up?"

"Forget the onions."

The phone clicks off.

Returning to the pepper disaster, I scramble after yellow, orange, red Bells, little Jalapenos, dark green Poblanos, pale green Anaheims, and bright orange Habaneros. Nothing as potent as a Ghost or Scorpion. I asked the Produce Manager if we could order Trinidad Moruga Scorpions, and he said *definitely not*. So I found them online.

I'm not tall enough to restack the pepper crates, so I leave them in several piles. Then I go back to chopping cabbage. I use red (purple really) for its magnificent color. Speaking of flamboyant, I wonder what effect it would have to add a Trinidad Scorpion to the Ranch dressing. The pepper is brilliant, orangey-red; I'd have to use the juice, rather than the pulp, so it's not detected. I watched a guy eat a Scorpion on YouTube. He popped the entire pepper into his mouth and chewed. The intensity kept building, until he could barely talk and started coughing, sweat pouring down his face, his eyes red and watering. Between spasms, he described torturous hot-cold sensations in the back of his throat. When he finally swallowed, his intestinal track went into convulsions. But the pepper didn't kill him. You'd have to eat three pounds of those things to die. I decide against lacing the Ranch dressing, because chances are they'd trace it back to me.

Before processing, I pull on fresh latex gloves. We've been extra careful since the salmonella outbreak. They think the bacteria originated in Produce. Probably the sprouts. (The Salad Bar no longer offers them.) Or it may have been passed by contaminated cantaloupe. (Always wash the rind.) At first they feared listeria—there was an outbreak a couple of years ago before I worked here. Listeria is more serious than salmonella.

Anyway, about twenty people in this town reported food poisoning. Chances are more people got sick, but the cases were unreported because people thought they had the flu or something else. Diarrhea, stomach cramps, fever, puking.

Nothing too terrible. Salmonella's pretty mild. Listeriosis, on the other hand, can spread to the nervous system causing loss of balance, confusion, convulsions, even death. Much more exciting.

I need to look into that.

I need to look into a lot of things. My mind, for example.

I don't feel guilty about Justus. Don't feel guilty about Ranger, or the college kid. Don't feel an ounce of guilt about that old lady I butchered with the chainsaw, or the tourist who drowned in the river, or the neighbor's stupid dog. And I don't feel guilty about Janet who got run over in the parking lot last night, when she was collecting carts.

Really, I don't give a damn.

But sometimes I think I *should*.

Sometimes I think a *normal* person would feel guilty.

And that stresses me out.

Stress is a silent killer.

Physical activity helps. According to the experts, physical activity releases endorphins, creating a natural high. So, when I feel stressed, I go to the gym, try a new recipe, or hack someone to pieces.

But the Justus thing nags me. In my mind's eye, I see him crashing on his bike, see blood gushing from his head, hear the screech of sirens as the ambulance rushes him to the hospital. But I can't remember if I threw that stone with my right hand or my left. I'm not even sure I hit him.

I intend to sort it out when I see Doctor A tomorrow. I've decided to call him Doctor A to keep our relationship friendly yet professional. I know Marcus wants to hook up with me. I can always tell. And I want to hook up with him, but you're not supposed to fuck your psychiatrist, are you? I guess some shrinks fuck their patients though. You read about those cases, see them on TV. Some psychiatrists specialize in sex therapy. I wonder if Marcus does, because I think sex is what I need.

I'm done with shredding cabbage and on the verge of slicing cucumbers.

Thinking about my appointment with Marcus, I grab a nice long cuke, pull down my pants, and shove it in.

Damn.

The thing is cold.

Liam slinks into Produce, and I quickly pull up my pants. He's too preoccupied to notice the bulge under my apron.

Meanwhile, the cucumber is warming up.

Glancing over his shoulder, to see if he's been followed, Liam says, "Lady wants a box of peaches."

I squeeze my thighs together, sucking in the cucumber. A moan escapes my mouth, and Liam glances at me.

"You okay?"

I nod, gripping the cucumber tighter, enjoying the pressure against my G-spot, the rush of heat.

Liam heads for the cooler.

Reaching my hand inside my pants, I slide the cuke in and out, in and out, rubbing the tip against my clit, tension building in my pelvis. I shove the cuke in deeper, pump faster, and bring myself to climax. Hot spasms shake my body. I collapse into the counter, staring at the colander of cucumbers, slip my big boy out—its green skin bruised and glistening—and toss the half-cooked cuke into the colander.

Liam appears carrying a crate of Palisade peaches.

"Find what you need?" I ask.

"Yeah."

Terri's voice comes over the intercom. "Liam, please dial 3-1-2."

Liam sets down the crate of peaches. Picks up the phone. Listens. Hangs up.

"What?" I ask.

"I'm getting written up."

"Again?"

"Strike three."

He grabs the peaches, kicks open the door.

In my book, Terri has too many strikes to count.

I give her the finger through the ceiling.

Returning to the cucumbers, I splash water over the colander. Thinking of Terri, I cut off the ends of each cucumber and run them through the processor, creating perfect slices. I wonder how efficiently the food processor would slice a finger. It might work well, if the finger were frozen—neat, little slivers. (I need to get a freezer, *bad*.) But slicing Terri's digits would be too simple. She deserves something more intense, something more exciting.

Something to get her juices flowing.

The cage.

I place the sliced cucumbers into a container, label it with the date. Then I wash the colander, the food processor, the machete and the chef's knife.

Time to chop more corn.

THERAPY

"TELL ME ABOUT YOUR CHILDHOOD." I'm sitting in the corner of a cushy couch across from Doctor A. He's ensconced behind his desk in a leather swivel chair, pen in hand, ready to take notes on a yellow pad of paper. (I didn't know they still make those.) Framed degrees and certificates are plastered on the gray wall behind him. Another wall holds shelves of books, not paperbacks—hardcovers. The guy must be a brainiac. He looks like he stepped out of a PBS miniseries, wearing tailored trousers instead of jeans, leather shoes that hold a shine rather than sneakers, a tie. (I bet it's silk.) *Quaint.* In this town, even businessmen wear spandex.

My legs are crossed and slanted to one side, displaying my calves to their best advantage, like I practiced in the mirror. I traded athletic shoes for fuck-me pumps, cherry red stilettos. A new skirt creeps up my thighs and I shift my position, encouraging its progress. I'm wearing no underpants.

Marcus—I mean, Doctor A—watches me intently, listening to every word I say. He seems to sincerely care. Poor man. He has no idea of who's sitting across from him. No idea how vulnerable he is right now. It's 5:30. I'm his last appointment of the day. The receptionist was gone when I arrived, so there are no witnesses. His office is in a small complex at the end of town and contains only a few occupants: an architect, a design consultant, a chiropractor who works three days a week (not today). At this hour, the other businesses have closed. The only car in the parking lot is his. I rode my bike and locked it up out back, so it can't be seen from the street.

"You said you felt powerless growing up, is that right, Sadie?"

My shoe slips from my foot and dangles from my toes. I swing it back and forth, hypnotizing Marcus.

"I don't want to talk about my childhood."

"What *do* you want to talk about?"

"Sex."

Marcus sets down his pen, leans back in his chair, loosens his tie, and then retightens it.

"You want to talk about the rape?"

I'm guessing he hasn't got any lately, maybe not since his wife croaked.

"Fuck me, Marcus."

"What did you say?" he leans toward me.

"I'm fucked up, Doctor A."

"In what way?"

"I want to kill people."

"We all feel that way sometimes."

"Really?"

"You need to take your power back."

I let my shoe drop from my foot and study Marcus through my lashes.

"Want some water?" He gets up, goes to a small refrigerator, pulls out two bottles. He opens one, takes a slug, and brings the other bottle around the desk to me. "What, exactly, do you remember about the rape?"

I take the bottle from him, allowing my hand to linger. He draws his hand away. Watching him, I twist off the cap, take a sip of water, and wipe my mouth. There's a red smear on my hand and, for a moment, I think it's blood. Then I remember that I'm wearing lipstick. Marcus is back behind his desk as if it offers some protection.

"I wasn't raped."

"Tell me what happened."

"I seduced that guy, drugged him, and fucked him with a cob of corn."

Marcus lowers the bottle from his mouth and studies me, the furrows on his forehead deepening. He sets the water bottle on his desk, picks up a piece of paper.

"According to the police report, what you've described is exactly what the rapist did to you."

"Blurred lines."

"What?"

"I like that song. You know it?"

I uncross my legs allowing my knees to part, enough to make sure he gets a good shot.

His gaze flicks to my crotch, then back to my face.

"What are you doing, Sadie?"

I spread my legs wider, my skirt creeping toward my waist. "Nothing."

I slip my hand between my thighs.

Standing, he leans into his desk. To support himself or to get a better view? I suspect both.

"I think we'd better end this now, Sadie."

I withdraw my hand, clap my legs shut, and pull my skirt toward my knees.

"I'll be a good girl, promise."

"I can refer you to someone else. Perhaps a woman—"

He glances at his phone, picks up the receiver.

"I want you."

I've come around the desk and stand behind him. I place my hand on his to stop him from dialing. Our touch is electric. Sparks fly, igniting a fire in my gut, so intense it races through my core, spreads through my chest into my arms and hands. My fingers burst into flames. My skin melts, dripping from the bones like wax. I press my breasts against his back, and feel his body tense as I breathe into his ear. Reaching around his chest, I unloosen his tie. Meanwhile, my tongue flicks at his neck. It would be easy to slip his tie off, wrap the silk around his throat, and pull it tight. But the muscles in his back tell me he's strong, and I don't think I can overpower him long enough to strangle him.

Besides, for his daughter's sake, I've promised not to kill him.

Even though it's tempting.

My eyes search his desk. A letter opener might work, but who uses them these days? The stapler could do some damage. My gaze lands on a framed photograph of Marcus and Carmela when she was about five.

I decide against the stapler.

"Must have been tough for Carmela to lose her mother so young," I say. "How did she die?"

"Who?"

"Your wife."

Marcus turns around to face me. Beads of sweat have formed along his hairline and he's breathing heavily.

"She didn't die. We're divorced."

"But the super said—" His face becomes a blur as I process the information. "You *divorced* Carmela's mom?"

This changes everything.

I brush my lips against his, feel his response.

He pulls away, but his pupils are dilated and he exudes a musky scent. I know he wants me.

"Sadie, please sit down. We can't do this."

"Why not?"

"Have you heard of the Hippocratic Oath?"

"Is that an oath for hypocrites?"

Before he can answer, I grab his hand and jam it in between my thighs, guiding his fingers between my swollen labia. Taking advantage of my newfound ambidexterity, I use my other hand to loosen his belt, undo the button of his pants, and pull down the zipper.

His cock is hard and smooth.

"What's your diagnosis, doctor?"

His breathing is rapid and shallow.

"B.P.D."

"What's that stand for? Big Pulsing Dick?"

"Borderline Personality Disorder."

His face is flushed, and sweat shimmers on his brow, but his forehead is smooth and unperturbed. I hear the whir of his brain, downloading and calculating—lots of power on his hard drive, definitely a gamer.

My fingers wrap around his joystick.

"Sadie, sit down."

"*You* sit down."

I press him into his leather swivel chair and climb on top of him.

This therapy is working.

His cock slips into me, a perfect fit. I ride him, my back arching as he slides in and out.

"You want it, bitch?"

Did I say that, or did he?

He turns up the voltage, rising from the chair, my cunt still hooked onto his cock. Heat courses through my body, my nerves on high-alert. Afraid to fall, I lock my legs around his back. He slams me against the wall, knocking down a framed diploma. His cock is a pneumatic hammer pounding my internal organs. Meanwhile, his forefinger and thumb vibrate my clit until I scream. He turns me around with mechanical precision, and I claw the wall as he comes in from behind. Jolts of electricity send shockwaves through my core, and I feel like I'm shattering into a thousand pieces.

I'm about to climax for the billionth time when something slips around my neck.

I can't breathe.

His tie is wrapped around my throat. I claw at the silk.

"Relax, Sadie."

I might relax if I could breathe.

He's pumping me so hard that I'm experiencing a nuclear reaction—my body convulsing with enough energy to start another universe.

I'd like to kick him in the balls.

I'm clutching at my throat, trying to release the pressure. Blood boils in my brain, my eyeballs bulging from their sockets, as my body explodes.

I come so hard, I'm blacking out.

The tie releases, and air rushes to my lungs as I collapse onto the carpet.

But he's not done.

He's on top of me, ripping the buttons from my shirt. Undoing my bra. The gold medallion swings around his neck, hypnotizing me. His chin feels rough against my chest as his teeth latch onto my nipple.

I kick, and that makes him more excited.

He flips me over, smashing my face into the carpet. Grabbing my wrists, he ties my hands behind my back.

I scream, even though no one will hear me.

He slaps silver tape over my mouth.

Rolls me onto my back.

I try to squirm out of his grasp, but he sits on my legs, holding me in place. Using scissors, he cuts my skirt from the hemline to the waist. Then he peels away the fabric, revealing my hips, my thighs, and my patch of pubic hair. Afraid to move, afraid of the harm the scissors might inflict, I lie still. He's using them like clippers, trimming my hair down to nothing. After he's done shaping, he snips around my labia. Satisfied, he sits back on his heels and examines his work.

I'm wondering if my insurance will cover this.

And will they go for nine more sessions?

Shoving my knees apart, he plunges his head between my thighs. I writhe uncontrollably as his tongue flicks at my clit. Parting my lips with his mouth, his tongue dives deeper, lapping up my juices.

I don't like feeling helpless, but with my hands tied and my mouth gagged, I don't have much recourse. Then an idea comes to me. I stop writhing, stop reacting. I relax and let go. My bladder releases.

Talk about pissing him off … he comes up gagging.

"Watersports?" Yellowish spit flies from his mouth. "You're into watersports?"

Kneeling on my legs, so I can't escape, he whips out his hose. I close my eyes against the shower of hot liquid. It seeps into my hair, runs down my neck and chest. Vomit rises to my mouth, but my lips are taped, so I swallow.

He shakes himself off. Gets up, freeing my legs.

I'm still wearing the stilettos, and I aim for his balls. But my aim is off, and my heel stabs his thigh.

"We're done," he says, ripping the tape from my mouth.

"I don't think so, Doctor."

I need a lot more therapy.

HE TOLD ME TO CALL his receptionist and make an appointment for next week. I told him I'm not sure I like his style of therapy. He mentioned something about giving it a chance, and then he wrote me a stronger prescription for Xanax.

Luckily, I worked out before the appointment, so I have my gym bag and a pair of shorts to wear home. You can bet I'm gonna make Doctor A pay for shredding my new skirt. The fuck-me shoes sure did their job. I kick them off and pull on my sneakers (Brooks Ravena 4s, black and purple as my throat). After submerging my head in the bathroom sink, I'm ready to face the evening. I'm heading out the door, when my phone rings.

I check the screen and see *Dad*.

I didn't pick up on his last three calls, and I've ignored my sister's threats (he's your dad too, call me or I'll have to lock him up) so guilt forces me to answer.

Before I can say hello, he yells, "Are you trying to poison me? This soup is fermented."

He must think I'm his aide. "Hi, Daddy, it's Sadie."

"What? Speak up. I can't hear you."

"It's Sadie."

"Sadie? Where are you?"

"In Colorado."

"What are you doing there?"

"I live here, remember?"

"This lentil soup you made is bad."

"I didn't make lentil soup."

"That's ridiculous. If you didn't make it, how can I be eating it?"

"Throw it out."

"That's a waste of food."

"Okay, then eat it."

"It's gone bad."

Our conversation goes like this for several minutes. He's still yelling when I hang up.

No cars in the parking lot, just my bicycle in back. The sun hasn't set, but clouds are moving in and I'm betting on a thunderstorm. It's cool enough for snow in the higher elevations; a blizzard in midsummer is not unheard of in the mountains. Down here we'll get rain. If I want to get home before the storm hits I should hurry, but when I reach the river, instead of heading toward the library and science museum, I turn toward Happy Valley old folks' home and coast along the bike trail, my eyes searching the thick brush that grows along the bank. I think I left the chainsaw somewhere along here the night I killed that old lady.

Twilight casts the world in shadow, and nothing is distinct; one line blurs into another. I hop off and walk, pushing my bike along the path. An old man is sitting on a bench outside the old folks' home, watching me. The same bench the old lady was sitting on. I must be getting close to where I dragged her corpse.

Corpse is a weird word, isn't it? Like corpuscle or corpulent.

Corpse.

Cadaver is even weirder.

Corpse. Cadaver. What's the diff?

Basically, a cadaver is a corpse destined for dissection, so if I want to be precise I should refer to the old lady as a cadaver.

Anyway, somewhere around here, I hacked her up.

School kids have knocked out the lights, so the trail is dark, but this spot looks familiar.

A clap of thunder makes me jump, and now it's drizzling.

I drop my bike behind a bush and leave the trail, beating a path through scrub oak and undergrowth, my legs getting jabbed by sticks and briars, my back damp from rain. I kick at a clump of fallen leaves, and uncover the remnants of a sneaker. (Cheap, a knock-off.) It's pink, like the sneaker that old lady wore. I shove more leaves aside, and something surfaces. At first, it looks like a branch, but when I look closer I wonder if it's a human femur. Anatomy class would come in handy now. The bone is chewed up, like some animal's been gnawing it. Bears frequent the river, so do wildcats and coyotes.

I get this creeped-out feeling someone's watching me.

I stand still, listening, but hear only the river and the rain.

I push through another stand of scrub oak and emerge close to the water. The rocks are slippery, and I almost lose my footing. Glancing down, I notice the glint of metal. My ex's chainsaw lies wedged between two rocks, half-buried in mud. The blade is bent and rusted, or maybe that's dried blood.

Grabbing the handle with both hands, I pry the saw loose and fall backward landing on my butt.

Stunned, I take a moment to recover.

A twig snaps in the brush behind me.

I glance toward the sound, expecting to see the gleaming eyes of a wild animal, but I see only the dark silhouette of scrub oak.

I stand slowly, holding the saw in front of me like a sword. I turn the power on, activate the choke, pull the starter, but nothing happens. Not even a sputter. Using the saw as a machete, I hack through the brush in the direction of my bicycle.

A hunched figure stands over my bike, reaching into the basket for my gym bag. As I emerge from the scrub oak, he looks up, and I recognize the old man from the bench. I hide the saw behind my back.

Supported by a cane, the old man takes a wobbly step toward me.

"You need help, young lady."

I'm not sure if it's question or a statement.

He stares at me, lips quivering, and reaches out a trembling hand. "Bad things happen on this trail at night."

"Like what?"

"Bad things."

A line of drool drips from his mouth and it annoys me. He's too old to be stumbling around in the dark, no less this rain. Too old to be alive.

Whipping out the saw, I charge him. Without power, it doesn't do much damage, but its weight knocks him to the ground. The impact stuns him, and he lies on the rocky earth. Tears in his eyes, he attempts to shield his face with trembling hands as I hit him with pepper spray—Trinidad Moruga Scorpion.

It must suck to be him: decrepit and alone, unable to defend himself.

"Old man, I'm doing you a favor."

My fingers wrap around a rock and I raise it. He cries out, his voice so weak, I think of a frightened rabbit as I bash in his skull.

Within minutes, the old man's a corpse—soon to become a cadaver.

Thanks to the broken saw, finishing the job takes longer than usual.

Today has been filled with challenges. Marcus said to take my power back, and his words inspire me to find my strength.

When I'm done, I place the chainsaw in the basket of my bicycle, toss my gym bag on top of the saw along with the old man's liver. Then I head home, contemplating what I'll make for dinner.

Recipe:
Sadie's Liver and Onions

If you're like me, you care about health and nutrition, and chances are you've heard about the Paleo Diet. It mimics the diet of our cavemen ancestors and includes vegetables, fruit, nuts, and plenty of meat. Natural meat, not the crap they try to feed us that's raised on an unnatural diet of corn. Did you realize that most commercial beef in the United States is *finished* with corn? (Meaning, the last few weeks of a cow's life it's fed corncobs that fatten up the meat and ulcerate the stomach, so the animal is bound to die a painful and unhealthy death.) Wild caught meat is best, but if that's not available go for grass-fed.

The Paleo Diet also recommends eating organ meats, like liver. Nutrient dense, liver is one of nature's super foods. Cooked correctly, liver has a tender, velvety texture. *The twist:* mushrooms. Yum!

Liver and Onions

Ingredients:
    1 liver, thinly sliced
    Juice of one lemon

1 large onion, sliced
1 cup mushrooms, sliced (preferably wild)
4 dried figs, chopped
¼ cup water
2 tablespoons balsamic vinegar
2 leaves of sage
½ cup butter
A little flour
Garlic powder
Sea salt
Fresh ground pepper

Preparation:
To slice liver easily: freeze it and then slice the meat when it's partially thawed. Marinate liver slices in lemon juice for 8-24 hours. (In the fridge or, in winter, out on the balcony.) After marinating, rinse the liver under the faucet and pat it dry. Season with salt and pepper. Then dredge in a little flour seasoned with salt, pepper, and garlic powder. Set aside.

Melt about ¼ cup butter, preferably in a cast iron skillet. Add the onions and turn heat to low. Cook onions at low heat until caramelized (about 45 minutes). Turn heat up to medium high, add more butter, then add the sliced mushrooms and cook till they release their juice. Add vinegar, water, and figs. Cook until the liquid evaporates, a few minutes. Remove from pan and set aside, keeping warm.

Add the rest of the butter to the skillet. Bring heat up, careful not to let the butter burn. The meat should sizzle when you place it in the pan. Sauté the liver for one minute, turn ONCE using tongs, and sauté for another minute. (Or less.) The outside should be brown and a bit crusty and the inside pinkish. DO NOT OVERCOOK.

Smother with onions and mushrooms. Enjoy.

Note: The Rocky Mountains offer a great variety of wild mushrooms. Mushrooms add earthy flavor and depth to a dish, and if you administer the right ones to aggravating people, mushrooms can rid your life of problems. Chanterelles are my favorite, golden colored. They're actually a fungus. You have to be careful because there are chanterelle look-alikes— if you're going for added intensity, pick the mushrooms with gills.

EXTERMINATOR

This past week, when I wasn't chopping onions, cucumbers, cabbage, and that old standby corn down in the dungeon, I spent my time at home in a cleaning frenzy—vacuuming, scrubbing, washing the curtains and the walls, bleaching the kitchen and the bathrooms, as if we're headed into spring instead of autumn. The place looks immaculate…cleaner anyway. Most of my furniture comes from the Humane Society Thrift Store (a great resource for animals), so my aesthetic is secondhand eclectic. New paint has done wonders. No trace of blood. I rearranged the couch, so it faces the fireplace and its back is to the kitchen. To create more space, I got rid of the coffee table. The place looks downright cozy. I might even get another cat or two.

Yesterday I took a trip to the mall and ordered a new chainsaw (donated the old one to the Humane Society) and a large chest freezer. (Chest freezer, LOL. What about arms and legs?) I was gonna go for the 8.8-cubic-feet Kenmore, but its capacity tops out at 308 pounds, and I think I need more storage, so I opted for the Kenmore Elite—24.9 cubic feet and it holds up to 827 pounds. Great features too, like Quick Freeze accelerated freezing, three lift-out baskets for better organization, an interior light and security lock. I even qualified for a Sears gold card—three months, no interest—I can pay it off fast, working overtime. The super says the covenants won't allow me to keep a freezer on the balcony. The sucker is too big anyway, but if I get rid of the table it will fit in the dining area. I can't wait for them to deliver it. The freezer in my fridge is so stuffed, I can barely close the door.

My only problem is the smell.

I sprayed the furniture with *Febreze,* and I rented a Rug Doctor carpet cleaner. Personally, I don't notice a bad odor, but the super said my neighbors have complained about the stink. I told her there must be a nest of squirrels in the walls—I hear them scurrying around at night—and I think some of them have died. She's called an exterminator, and he's scheduled to come tomorrow morning, so I need to finish cleaning out the closets before he starts snooping around.

What won't fit into trash bags, I'll burn in the fireplace. The nights are cooling off, so I don't think a fire will seem strange. Did you know that pine cones make good kindling? We have a lot of those lying around the courtyard. And rendered body fat is a great accelerant.

I'm down in the courtyard, collecting pine cones in a plastic bag, when the cop car pulls into the parking lot. After exchanging niceties with the super, Gorski and Redbear stroll into the courtyard acting like they own the place.

Hoping they won't notice me, I crawl under low hanging branches of a blue spruce, narrowing my search for cones.

"Mrs. Bardo, may we have a word?"

I act surprised when I see Gorski hovering over me. Redbear stands beside him, scribbling on his notepad.

"Oh, hi," I say, wiping pine needles off my yoga pants and avoiding Gorski's gaze. I get up, holding my bag of cones, and (careful to use my left hand) hold the bag out to the cops. "Did you know these make good kindling?"

Ignoring this choice piece of information, Gorski says. "We have a few more questions, ma'am."

"About what?"

"Justus Johnson. We have reason to believe someone hit him deliberately."

"A car crashed into him on purpose?"

"A rock."

"Really?" The bag of pine cones slips from my hand, and I fall to my knees retrieving them.

Gorski kneels beside me, picks up a cone and hands it to me, forcing eye contact.

Redbear continues scribbling.

Gorski says, "The angle of trajectory shows the alleged rock hit him from above as if someone threw it from a balcony."

"You think he was murdered?"

I try to control my shaking hand as I pick up another cone.

"Murdered? No, ma'am. I didn't mention murder."

"But if someone threw the rock ..." My voice trails off.

Shut-up. Shut-up. Shut-up.

"Just covering our bases," Gorski says. "We're working with the store's insurance company, investigating the alleged accident."

What *exactly* does alleged mean? Something like suspected, supposed, unproved.

I reach for another pinecone and it pricks me.

"Ouch." I suck my bleeding finger.

"Careful, ma'am, those things are sharp."

I don't like the way Gorski eyes me. I glance at Redbear, and he stops writing.

"Can we talk over at the picnic table, ma'am? I'd like your undivided attention."

"Sure."

I collect my bag of pinecones and follow the officers.

After we sit down, I ask, "Am I a suspect?"

Gorski's eyes bore into mine. "You're right handed?"

"Left."

Redbear consults his notes. "That's what she said last time, and the Produce Manager confirmed it."

"You spoke to my boss?"

"Like I said, we're covering our bases," Gorski says. "According to forensics, the person who threw the stone is right handed."

"I'm a lefty."

"So you said." Gorski glances at Redbear, then turns back to me. "You're off the hook, for now."

"*For now?* What does that mean?"

"Chances are Mr. Johnson's insurance company will want to talk to you."

"Why?"

"Speaking from experience, insurance companies don't hand out money easily. Before they pay hospital expenses, they'll make certain there's no extenuating circumstances— like an unknown party who's libel for the accident. This kind of case usually involves an investigation."

Redbear closes his pad and both cops stand.

I follow them to the parking lot, watch as their car drives away. Then, clutching my bag of pinecones, I run upstairs and start a fire.

I'M DRAGGING THE LAST BAG of garbage down to the dumpster when an unfamiliar SUV pulls into the parking lot. It's shiny and undented, unlike the vehicles of most residents. The door swings open, and high heels attached to slender legs encased in pantyhose swing onto the pavement. They belong to a redhead who's carrying a classy briefcase—real leather, not simulated. Around here, if there's a weirder sight than a man wearing a tie, it's a woman in a business suit.

I, on the other hand, fit right in, wearing stained yoga pants, a sweaty tee-shirt and lemon yellow running shoes (Adidas, Avanti 2s, sale-priced online at Zappos). The yoga pants and tee-shirt are black, so blood that oozed from the last trash bag I heaved into the dumpster is barely noticeable, but there's a red blotch on my left shoe. If the subject of stains comes up, I'll claim they're ketchup. I'm making hamburgers for dinner, so the story fits. I know, I know, hamburgers are usually beef, but this guy was an actor in the local community theater—thought he was the next Bryan Cranston or something. Anyway, these burgers are truly *ham*.

The high heels click toward me as I lower the cover of the dumpster, and *I* click into Sadie the Sadist mode.

"Excuse me," the woman says. "I'm looking for Unit 20."

"I'm Unit 20."

"Sadie Bardo?"

I nod.

Lowering designer sunglasses, she peers at me, her gaze lingering on my shoe.

"Ketchup."

"What?"

"The stain. I'm making hamburgers for dinner."

"Tory Hartmann, claims adjuster for Insurance Alliance." She extends her hand, perfectly manicured, then quickly pulls it back when she notices the black funk beneath my fingernails.

Her hair reminds me of Natalia Romanova's in *The Avengers*, so shiny red I want to tear it out. It's swept into an elegant chignon, held in place by a fancy comb that looks like real tortoiseshell, not plastic. By comparison, my hair looks like my mop at work after sopping up spilled carrot juice.

"Nice glasses," I say. "What's the brand?"

"Louis Vuitton. Is there somewhere we can talk?"

"About what?"

"Justus Johnson. I believe you worked with him?"

"Justus Johnson." I frown, pretending to mull over the name. "Oh, yes. From the supermarket."

"You must know about the accident."

"I heard about it. Tragic."

"Are you willing to answer a few questions?"

"Sure. My place is upstairs."

Her heels click behind me as she follows me along the path into the courtyard, then up the stairway to my apartment.

I open the door and when she steps inside I notice her nose wrinkling.

"Dead squirrels," I say. "The exterminator comes tomorrow."

She nods. "I had skunks under my deck."

"Want a burger? I'm about to fry them up."

A propane grill is another item on my wish list, but where would I put it?

"Sorry to interrupt your dinner. This shouldn't take much time." She motions to the couch. "May I?"

"Sure. Something to drink? I can offer you cranberry juice, Diet Pepsi, or—this must be your last call of the day, would you like a glass of wine?"

"Water would be great."

"The tap water tastes like sulfur. How about cranberry juice?"

"Sounds good."

I grab a glass from the cabinet, where I also keep the Unisom. That stuff comes in handy, but the economy-sized bottle I lifted from Wal-Mart is nearly finished. I wasn't expecting company.

"Ice?"

"No thanks."

I squeeze the contents of five gelcaps into a glass and top it off with juice. The new arrangement of my furniture makes it easy to avoid detection. Settled on the couch, the insurance adjuster faces the fireplace, her back to me. Her red head bows over her briefcase as she extracts papers.

"May I call you Tory?" I call from the kitchen.

"Sure."

"Live around here?"

"Denver."

"Long drive."

"Yeah."

I bring her the glass of juice.

Her gaze meanders over my stained tee-shirt.

"I'm such a klutz, darned ketchup squirted all over me."

Smiling, she takes a sip of cranberry. Her lips pucker at the taste.

"It's unsweetened," I say. "Want some sugar?"

"Unsweetened is healthier." She takes another sip, stares at the dying embers in the fireplace. "It's warm out there today. You had a fire?"

"I'm cold-blooded." I laugh nervously. "That suit you're wearing must be hot. Why don't you take off your jacket?"

"Thanks. I will."

She folds the jacket, lining out, as if my ketchup stains might be contagious. I notice the Armani label.

"I'll hang it up for you."

"Thanks."

Noting that we wear the same size, I find a place in the hall closet, next to my shabby winter coat.

"So, you work for the insurance company?"

"They hire me. I'm an independent agent."

She runs her fingers through her annoying hair.

"On the road a lot?" I ask.

"All I do is drive."

"Must be tough on your family."

"I'm single."

"Me too," I say. Chances are, she already knows that. This lady is no fool. I warn myself to tread carefully. "So you're heading back to Denver tonight?"

"Yes, but I'm in no hurry. I plan to do the scenic loop and spend the night in Ouray."

"Good plan. The hot springs are fantastic. And the drive is gorgeous. Treacherous though—hairpin turns on mountain passes. Be careful."

I pick up her empty glass and go back to the kitchen to refill it. Only three more SleepGels. I consider breaking out my Xanax, but I hate to waste the good stuff on a stranger.

Tory sorts through papers, arranging them on the couch, since I no longer have a coffee table. Then she pulls out an iPad.

"Mrs. Bardo—"

"Call me Sadie, please."

"*Sadie*, I want to tie up a few loose ends."

I hand her the replenished glass. She places it on the side table, next to her sunglasses. I thought about getting rid of that table too, but it doesn't take up much room. Anyway, it holds the lamp I use for reading.

I perch on the edge of a frayed easy chair that I inherited from my father, catty-corner to Tory.

Her smile reveals perfect teeth.

"Did you witness the accident?"

"Accident?"

"Justus Johnson—"

"No, I didn't."

"Really?" She shuffles through her papers, then flicks on her iPad. "According to the initial police report, you weren't *certain* if you witnessed the accident. Can you tell me more about that?"

This woman is way too sharp.

Careful to use my left hand, I nudge the glass of cranberry juice toward her.

She picks it up and sips, her eyes focused on me.

"Did you, or did you not witness the accident?"

"I was on pain pills at the time. I don't remember much."

"So you were home at the time of the accident."

"Like I told the police, I couldn't work due to an injury."

"A cut on your left hand."

"My thumb. Nine stitches."

I show her the scar.

"That must have hurt."

"Not on painkillers."

"So, at the time of the accident, you were sitting on your balcony?"

"I don't remember."

Tory consults her iPad. "According to the police report, you were on your balcony when Justus Johnson had the accident."

"I can't see the bike path if I'm sitting."

"Were you standing?"

"I don't remember."

"Don't remember if you were standing when you saw the accident?"

I don't like the way this is going. She needs to drink up.

I head back to the kitchen, find a bag of veggie chips (no corn or soy), dump them into a bowl. Strategically, I place the salty chips on the side table next to Tory.

She nibbles one. Follows it with a gulp of juice.

"So," she says, her voice sounding a bit thick, her cadence slowing, "you were standing on your balcony that morning when you noticed Mr. Johnson riding his bicycle?"

"Maybe. He rides to work every day."

Tory glances at me, her eyes less sharp than earlier. "You pay attention to his patterns?"

"No."

Her synapses might be decelerating, but she almost trapped me.

"You just said he rides to work every day."

"Everybody knows that."

"Do they?" She takes another sip of juice. "Since your left hand was wounded at the time, did you come to rely on your right?"

Without benefit of alcohol, the Unisom isn't working fast enough.

"Please answer my question, Sadie. Did the accident you suffered to your left hand force you to become proficient with your right?"

I get up from my chair and wander to the fireplace where coals still glow within the ash. Using my right hand, I pick up the iron poker and stir the embers. I prod what appears to be a remnant of the actor's humerus. Finding that humorous, I chuckle.

"Did I say something funny, Sadie?"

"Yes."

I whirl toward Tory, wielding the hot poker, the glowing tip aimed at her gaping mouth. Before she says another word, I charge her, the weight of my body propelling me forward as I ram the poker between her lips, smashing her white teeth. The poker spears her throat like a javelin. The point lodges in the base of her skull and pins her to the couch. Blood gushes from her mouth. She tries to scream and makes a gurgling sound.

"Any more questions?"

She stares at me with frightened eyes.

"I'll take your silence as a no."

I rip the cord from my reading lamp and use it to secure her wrists. Her eyes bulge as I straddle her. Blood pulses from her wound, splattering my face. Tastes like an iron supplement. I hope she doesn't have AIDS.

Note to self: *Head wounds bleed excessively.*

I wonder if the stains on the couch will be permanent, and what about my newly cleaned carpet? Thank goodness I haven't returned the Rug Doctor.

The poker has severely damaged her spinal cord.

Her head moves from side-to-side, as she struggles to breathe, but her arms and legs seem paralyzed. I grab her iPad and Google *spinal injuries.*

According to this diagram, the poker is lodged in the high cervical nerves of the spinal cord, C1—C4, which explains why she's shit her pants. C1—C4 injuries often lead to paralysis of the arms and legs, and pretty soon she'll stop breathing. I'm angry with myself because, if she's paralyzed, I didn't need to destroy my reading lamp by ripping out the cord to tie her wrists.

Essentially, she's already dead.

This website says, if I could provide her with mechanical ventilation, I could keep her alive for quite some time. That might be fun. With mechanical ventilation, she'd be able to breathe and swallow, even speak. Of course, without proper planning, I lack the equipment. That's why I don't like unexpected company. Now I'm stuck with this body, this half-dead corpse. It says here, the major cause of C1—C4 injuries is traffic accidents. That's useful information.

A buzzing sound interrupts my reading. Tory's cell phone is vibrating, and the screen says *Office.* I give the caller time to leave a message, then I check her voice mail.

Hey, Tor. See you Monday. We need to discuss your progress on the Johnson case.

I text back: *Drivving 2 Uray now. Bardo clear. Jonson kase a wash.*

Get back a text: *Don't text and drive!*

I relay the message to Tory, "Don't text and drive."

Her head has stopped moving, and foam bubbles from her lips. The comb has slipped out from her chignon, allowing loose strands to fall into her face.

I wish I had that head of hair.

I consult the iPad. There's controversy regarding this topic, but according to *Wikipedia,* Native Americans learned how to scalp from Europeans. The Iroquois took up the practice with a vengeance. Doesn't mention our local tribe, the Southern Utes.

Peeling the skin from the skull without ruining the hair is a challenge. The hair is caked with blood. Needs a good wash and conditioner. When I've finished scalping Tory, to avoid excessive dripping and spatter, I employ my Courtesy Clerk skills and double bag her head.

Conveniently, her car keys and her wallet are in her briefcase. I plan to pull her SUV around to the walkway when it's dark and people are holed-up in their condos, glued to their flat screens. Then I'll drag the body down the stairs, wrapped in a tarp, of course, dump it in the wheelbarrow the super uses for gardening, and wheel it to the SUV. After the corpse is loaded (this one is definitely a corpse, not a cadaver, unless you count scalping as dissection), I'll throw my bike in back. The road to Ouray is steep and winding, rocky ravines off the shoulders, hairpin switchbacks without guardrails, but it's mostly downhill coming back. Not many people travel it at night.

I know the perfect spot to stage an accident.

I Google: *making a car explode,* and a quick search informs me that the impact from plunging several hundred feet onto jagged rock should sever the fuel line and damage the tank enough to make the SUV go up in flames. A full tank of fuel should ensure a serious inferno. I'll buy gas, using Tory's credit card, before we head up the mountain. According to this article (and shows I've watched on TV) it takes a long time to incinerate a body, but even if the SUV doesn't explode, the corpse should burn enough to eradicate evidence.

Meanwhile, I'll clean up this mess and fry a burger.

CYBERNETICS

K RISTA TEXTED ME AGAIN. SHE and Tracy want to meet at The Quiet Lady for happy hour next Friday. I can't go. I have to work that evening. Besides, I'm not up for the Dynamic Duo. Krista says she's worried about me. I never showed for anatomy class. Apparently, that put her do-gooder gene into a tailspin and, I know from experience, if I keep ignoring her she'll get more persistent. But I haven't texted back. I don't know what to say to her, so I'll pretend her message got lost in cyberspace.

I love cyberspace. It's nebulous. Tactile communication gets sticky, messy, and way too personal.

That's why I've been avoiding Marcus. (Since our session, I can't bring myself to call Marcus *Doctor anything*.) When I see him, in the parking lot of our complex or down in the courtyard, I hide. The guy might think I'm Borderline, but he's psycho.

I think about him all the time.

Despite his unorthodox methods, or maybe because of them, he *gets* me. It's like he sneaks inside my head, peers into dark corners and sees stuff *I* don't even notice. In other words, he gives good head.

Okay, I admit it. I'm attracted to his brain. I guess you could call it a biochemical obsession. Our programming synchs, our synapses connect, we're tuned to the same frequency. We don't need the Internet, 4G, Facetime, or smoke signals to communicate.

Wouldn't it be great if brains could live forever?

There's this scientist/techie guy, Ray Kurweil, who says by 2040 we'll be able to upload our brains to a computer. I figure by 2041 we'll all be robots. So if you make it to the 2040s, you'll never get decrepit like my father.

He left me another weird message. About socks. Apparently his are all mismatched, so he's forced to wear brown with blue, but that's not what bothers him. What bothers him is he's *afraid* of socks, hates wearing them because they smother his feet and his soul can't breathe. It's not the first time that I've heard this complaint. On several occasions I've tried to explain it's soles, not souls, but he insists his life force permeates his body through the bottom of his feet. When I've suggested he forget about the socks and go without, he tells me if he goes sockless his shoes will become angry and trample him.

I'm hoping for a stampede.

My phone beeps, notification that I've received yet another text from Krista: *Yes or no?*

She gets like that, demanding. If I don't text her back, she'll keep texting till I say yes. Or worse, she'll call me. I don't have time to talk, don't *want* to talk to her. I'm busy stalking Marcus.

To get Krista off my back, I text: *Werk Fday.*

Speaking of Marcus, his receptionist called yesterday wanting to schedule my next appointment. Guess the insurance went through. Who knew they cover getting fucked.

For the past week I've been doing surveillance, observing the courtyard. Today I've been watching from my living room all morning, standing at the picture window, hidden by the curtain. Sometimes Marcus comes home for lunch. If he doesn't show up soon, chances are I won't see him today, because it's almost time for me to go to work. I know the time without glancing at the clock, because the mail lady—mailwoman, whatever she's called—is down in the courtyard stuffing letters into the open mouths of postboxes. Wondering if there's any mail for me, I head downstairs to check.

Today is one of those crisp, blue sky Colorado days. On days like this I want to ride my bike through the valley, cruise along the river, blow off work. It sucks to be responsible.

I say hi to the postmistress (I think that's her official title) and unlock my letterbox. I'm shuffling through bills and advertisements when I hear my name. Turning, I see Marcus.

He looks good—clean shaven and neatly pressed. *Damn.* Why do my legs feel like gummy worms? Would I feel this uncomfortable sensation in my gut if I were a robot? I don't think so. If I were a simulacrum, the synthetic humans Philip Dick writes about, would I be short-circuiting? Being a real person sucks. My stomach's doing somersaults and making strange noises. I wonder if I'm hungry.

Lowering my new Louis Vuitton sunglasses, I give Marcus the seductive look I've been practicing.

His eyes sparkle with amusement.

"Nice shades, Sadie. Have you been avoiding me?"

I shake my head.

"You haven't called my office."

This morning I did body maintenance—washed the hair, applied mascara to the lashes, glossed the lips—so Sadie's looking good. Now I'm working on her programming, so her image matches what comes out of her mouth.

Arching an eyebrow (do you know how much practice it takes to arch *one* eyebrow?), I say, "I want you to be my friend."

"Of course I'm your friend, Sadie."

"I want you to be my *friend*."

The sparkle in his eyes dims.

"I don't think that's a good idea."

"Why not?"

"You're my *patient*."

"I quit therapy." Avoiding his gaze, I shuffle through my mail. Two credit card statements, an advertisement from a car dealership, and the new *Victoria's Secret* catalogue. Hiding the catalogue under bills, I change the subject, "Where's Caramel?"

"In California with her mother. She gets Carmela for the school year. I get her for the summer and Christmas. Why have you quit therapy?"

"That must be difficult for Caramel."

"I think you should give the process a chance."

"It sucks, not having two parents."

"She *has* two parents, Sadie."

The more uncomfortable he looks, the more at ease I feel.

"Why do you think your marriage failed?"

"Why does any marriage fail?" Marcus glances at his watch. "I've got to go—"

"Come over for dinner Wednesday?"

"I don't think—"

"I'm a good cook."

"I know, but—"

Victoria Secret slips from my hands and falls onto the ground. A woman in a lace bra and thong looks up from the lawn. Before I can grab it, Marcus scoops up the catalogue and hands it back to me. Our fingers touch.

"Just a neighborly supper. Six thirty?"

"All right, I'll stop by for a little while."

He walks toward the parking lot, hesitates, keeps walking.

I watch his ass and wonder, if I use priority shipping, will my purchase arrive before our dinner date?

The spell breaks when my cell phone rings.

"Hi, Daddy."

"I can't find my shoes."

"Have you tried the closet?"

No point in mentioning that I haven't been to his place since Christmas. My last visit did not go well. When I cooked him dinner, he spat out the meat and accused me of poisoning him. When I was a kid, he used to do that to my mother. No doubt she would have killed him, if he hadn't killed her first. Anyway, I'm not a fan of Phoenix. It's a giant traffic jam and hot as hell. No wonder my father moved there. It suits him.

He's yelling about loafers.

I'm not sure if he's referring to me, or shoes, but I hang up.

I RODE MY BIKE TO work as usual, and clouds rolled in without warning, so I got caught in the rain. Colorado is like that in August, clear mornings, cloudy afternoons, and then it pours all night. No one complains, because we need the moisture. But now I'm wet.

As I walk into the store, I notice a display of corn outside, another at the entrance, a third by cut fruit in Produce.

The remodel is nearly finished. The Grand Opening is scheduled to coincide with Labor Day weekend at the end of the month, two weeks from now. The construction crew is done with Deli, Bakery, Meat, and now they're working in Produce—switching out the floor from concrete to wood for the rustic look, replacing display cases, remodeling shelves. They've installed a new sprinkler system for the wet rack. Now, every time you try to grab a bag of carrots or head of lettuce, you risk a thunderstorm. Happens to me all the time when I check sell-by dates.

The Produce Manager keeps adding jobs to my routine—checking sell-by dates and doing markdowns, facing lettuce, and now I'm in charge of dried fruit and nuts. He told me raisins are my *number one* priority. First thing each day, I'm supposed to grab the cart and work the back stock, which means fill holes and use a handheld scanner to determine what we've got and what we need to order. It's a big responsibility. And, frankly, it's a challenge.

Most produce carts are sturdy, so they can support heavy boxes of onions, potatoes, squash, macho stuff that requires muscle to stock. At all times these carts *must* carry a crate of bananas (our number one seller), a spray bottle of water, and box of paper towels for cleaning. Not my cart. The fruit and nut cart is a cockeyed U-boat stacked with off-kilter, mismatched boxes: raisins, prunes, almonds, peanuts, rice crackers, apricots—stuff none of the guys want to work. Too gay, I guess. Thanks to the remodel, dried fruit has been relegated to an aisle far from Produce, next to oatmeal. Consequently, I have to roll my tipsy cart across the store, weave through people and displays, and hope a crate of *Craisins* doesn't tumble off and knock out a customer.

Planning my strategy for the day, I walk, head down—my sneakers (red Converse All Stars) squeaking, thanks to the rain inside and out—and run into the Produce Manager. Literally. He's crawling around the floor by the berry display. At first I think he's looking for a contact lens or something, but then I realize he's tracking wayward labels.

"Change in plans," he says without looking up.

"I know, raisins and nuts. I'm about to get the cart."

"Forget nuts. Corn."

My shoulders sag.

"How much?"

He grunts, attempting to peel a label off the floor.

"As much as you can do. Olathe is big. Very big. Customers can't get enough." He pulls out a box cutter, distends the razor, and points the blade at a trough of corn. "I've filled that bin ten times today, set that trash can next to it so people can shuck their own. Gonna be this way through the Grand Opening and Labor Day."

"Maybe we should plant a cornfield in the middle of the store, so customers can pick their own and enjoy the full corn experience."

He stops scraping, considers my idea, then says, "Chop, chop."

The doctor (not Marcus, a *real* doctor) gave me braces to hold my wrists in correct alignment, and they help. My hands have stopped going numb at night, but when I cut corn, the vibration from chopping kinks my neck and makes my fingers tingle. You might imagine I'm unhappy—delegated to standing on cold concrete, wearing wet sneakers, cutting corn all day—but I'm too excited about my dinner date with Marcus tomorrow evening to be bummed. In fact, I feel elated.

Riding the elevator down to the dungeon, I plan the menu. Perhaps an aphrodisiac. Oysters on the half shell with a squeeze of cunt juice for an appetizer? Asparagus spears, creamy avocado, and deviled eggs for the main course, served with a sauce of garlic, basil, and fresh come? Nipples dipped in chocolate for dessert…

I'm humming along to some disco ditty from the 1970s, feeling ecstatic, but my mood shifts when I enter the work area. Some guy I've never seen before is standing at the sink up front where Liam should be crisping vegetables. This guy is about 6 foot 5 and must weigh close to three hundred pounds. He's wearing shorts and a plastic yellow apron, hosing down Romaine lettuce. Behind him, there's a cart stacked with bins of broccoli, cilantro, parsley, and leeks.

"Where's Liam?" I ask. "On vacation?"

"You could say that. He's gone."

"Gone where?"

"Fired."

The goliath plunges a head of lettuce into a vat of icy water.

I gasp, like I'm drowning.

"When?"

"Yesterday."

"Why?"

"Insubordination. Refused to use the intercom. They wrote him up."

"Who?"

"Terri, I think."

Just as I suspected.

Terri the Terrible.

This calls for action. Nothing short of revolution. Terri has nothing on Marie Antoinette. I grab the guillotine, stomp to my corner, no longer shivering and cold, but steaming. I slam an RPC of corn onto the stainless steel counter, preparing to decapitate.

Chop, chop, chop.

Shuck, shuck, shuck.

Fuck, fuck, fuck.

I want to kill someone.

I want to kill *a lot* of people.

Not only Terri the Terrible, but the Produce Manager who's so busy scraping labels off the floor that he let Liam get fired, and that hulk washing lettuce nonchalantly. I want to kill the entire store, the entire corporation—an evil empire conspiring to control the food supply, force-feeding the population genetically engineered soy and corn designed to convert our DNA and transform us into robot slaves. They're in bed with the government. It's a worldwide conspiracy.

Pressure builds inside my head. My brain aches. I stop chopping, lean against the counter. Gray matter oozes from my ears, eyes, mouth, nostrils as my mind expands, pushing the boundaries of my skull until my head explodes. Neurons shoot threads of light through my consciousness linking me to a network so complex, so vast and powerful, by comparison the World Wide Web seems as archaic as television. Commands are dispatched directly to my cerebrum, reprogramming circuits, mutating neurotransmitters, rebuilding pathways and transforming me into an entity beyond human.

Chop, chop, chop.

They're planning a grand event to coincide with Labor Day.

Chop, chop, chop.

A directive will be transmitted, initiating activation.

Chop, chop, chop, chop, chop.

Surveillance must be vigilant.

Due to the remodel, management is on high alert, working in conjunction with government agencies. The FDA, CIA, FBI, and highly secretive CORN (Corporate Operatives Reordering Neuropathy). As the Grand Opening approaches, spies drop in unannounced to check on the store's progress. The new guy washing lettuce is obviously an operative.

Sent to terminate subversives like Liam.

Like me.

I grab another crate of corn.

Chop, and chop, and f@#king chop.

Timing is everything.

Speaking of timing, scheduling the Grand Opening to coincide with Labor Day raises the temperature of my thermostat to boiling. *Labor* Day is supposed to be a holiday to honor laborers—not bosses. The store should be closed for business, throwing a picnic for its workers—at least providing a day of rest so our systems can be updated. Instead, while corporate big shots loll around the pool or lake, drinking and barbequing, employees will be slaving away in basements. No double-time, not even time-and-a-half. Holiday pay is obsolete. Ten years from now, if you're not a robot slave, you won't have a job.

I wonder how Liam's going to pay his rent.

I'd like to give him a going away present. A robot. Nothing elaborate. Just a simple bot with a quiet personality. A bot who could do his job—stocking vegetables and fruit, removing the rotten stuff from bins, helping customers locate leeks and ginger root. A bot who wouldn't mind speaking on the intercom and who'd bring the paycheck home to Liam.

I've been watching videos on YouTube. Robots are advancing fast. Some fly, some walk, others look like crabs or snakes. Amazon delivered my new waterproof, hot pink vibrator in less than fifteen minutes using a flying drone. (Good thing; I needed it for an emergency.) And the Japanese have developed humanoids that look like people. They plan to replace us ASAP. That's where this store is heading. That's what they want us to be. Humanoids who'll work around the clock for nothing. No complaints. Humanoids who don't demand insurance. Bots with an extended warranty, because this place will overload them until they short-circuit.

In a year or two, when robots take over, I'm not sure how I'll earn a living. Maybe Corporate will give us an option to convert, to upload our brains into our replacements.

Maybe that's already happened.

If a robot kills a human, who's responsible? The owner? The manufacturer? The programmer?

Chop, chop, chop.

A robot can't be held accountable.

Recipe:
Sadie's Aphrodisiac Ragoût

Ragoût, a well-seasoned stew of meat and vegetables, is a French term, meaning "to revive the taste." Who knows more about food and sex than the French? So, when you want to rev the action in your bedroom, try this tasty aphrodisiac. For a bigger bang, I've taken a traditional recipe and made a few choice substitutions.

Aphrodisiac Ragoût

Ingredients:
   1 pound penises (I prefer fresh over frozen)
   Freshly ground black pepper
   2 tablespoons olive oil (extra virgin, natch)
   5 tablespoons butter
   1 pound mixed mushrooms, cleaned
   1 medium shallot, chopped fine
   ½ teaspoon Dijon mustard
   1 teaspoon Herbs d' Provence
   ½ cup vermouth
   ½ cup heavy cream
   Salt

Come (to taste)

Spritz of cunt juice

Preparation:

Preheat oven to 400 degrees Fahrenheit.

Season whole penises with salt and pepper. Meanwhile heat a large, cast iron skillet on medium-high heat. When skillet is hot, add oil and heat till simmering, then add one tablespoon of butter. When butter has melted, add penises, sear, browning like sausages. Transfer skillet to the oven and roast for about ten minutes. Remove penises to a cutting board, tent with foil, and let meat rest for another ten minutes.

Meanwhile, cut the mushrooms into quarters. Heat 2 tablespoons butter in the skillet over medium-high heat, making sure butter doesn't burn. Add the mushrooms, and increase heat to high. Let mushrooms brown, then turn. Add more butter if the pan seems dry. Add the shallot and sauté for about two minutes. Season with salt, pepper, mustard, and Herbs d' Provence. Pull pan from heat, and add vermouth. Return pan to heat, and scrape any brown bits from bottom with a spoon. Add cream. Bring to a boil. Remove from heat.

Jerk off.

Stir in fresh come.

Slice penises crosswise, and arrange on a platter. Smother with mushrooms. Top with a spritz of cunt juice, and serve with a side of asparagus.

DINNER DATE

THE CURTAINS ARE DRAWN AND evening light filters through the blood red fabric, casting a warm glow on my apartment. I'm streaming love songs on Pandora—mid-twentieth century stuff my dad might play by Frank Sinatra and Tony Bennett—the kind of songs you'd hear in a classy restaurant.

I'm hoping the music will put Marcus in the mood.

Since my conversion, I have trouble relating to anything romantic. Truthfully, I no longer see the point of having sex with other people. It's an act best executed alone, a measure taken for self-maintenance to ensure all circuits are performing. I jerked off earlier, while preparing dinner, and the outcome proved more than satisfactory. Truthfully, the idea of sex for procreation seems random and messy ... obsolete.

But, for the sake of scientific research, I've set the stage for a romantic evening. And I have a hunch fucking with Marcus will reawaken my libido.

Dinner's simmering on the stove. I've popped open a bottle of Shiraz and thrown a tablecloth over the chest freezer, so the food can be served buffet style. I even lit candles. And I've sharpened all the knives.

I'm wearing the Black Widow jumpsuit I bought online, had it shipped overnight. It's more provocative than anything I saw in the *Victoria's Secret* catalogue, made of stretchable Pleather that hugs my curves. I washed and styled the red hair I took off that snotty insurance adjuster, and I'm wearing her scalp. (I tried to pin her hair into a chignon, but had to settle on a bun.) Knee high black boots add the finishing touch. I gaze into the mirror, turning one way, then another, admiring my transformation. Natalia Romanova, check me out. Sadie the Sadist is the newest and baddest Avenger.

I wish my left knee would stop shaking.

My system is on overload. I need to reboot, but there's no time.

Marcus will be arriving soon.

To calm my nerves, I pop another Xanax and wash it down with wine. In some ways, I'm still human.

I head back to the living room, push aside the curtain and peer into the courtyard.

No sign of Marcus.

Two young mothers stand by the sandbox, talking, while their kids run around. I recognize the little girl from downstairs, one building over. She's making a ruckus, driving her pink battery-operated car around the cement walkway. A boy on a bicycle cuts in front of her, and she honks her horn.

Marcus should be here any minute.

The pink car crashes into the bike. The boy, the bike, the car and girl careen off the walkway.

My doorbell rings.

How did Marcus sneak by me?

I run to the entryway, press my eye against the peephole. Despite the double dose of Xanax, my stomach is flip-flopping like a hooked trout. I wish that fish would hurry up and die. Gorski and Redbear stand on my doorstep. Gorski leans toward the door and his eyeball peers into mine.

I consider my options:

1. Pretend I'm not here and hope they go away—fat chance, since Gorski just gave me an eye exam.

2. Hurry to the bedroom, jump off the balcony and run—I'll probably break a leg.

3. Open the door and find out what they want.

"Officers, what can I do for you?"

"Evening, Mrs. Bardo. Please open the door."

Reluctantly, I undo the chain.

"Hope we're not interrupting—"

Gorski's gaze travels to my cleavage.

I zip up the jumpsuit.

"Actually, I'm expecting company."

"This won't take long."

Dean Martin is singing "Volare," the upbeat tune a sharp contrast to my current mood. I glance at the living room, making sure I haven't forgotten to put something away like a bloody chainsaw. The officers step inside. The three of us stand cramped together in the small foyer while Dean croons about happy hearts and wings.

Redbear takes out his notepad and a pen. He's switched to ink; this must be getting serious. His mustache has filled out since the last time I saw him. It reminds me of a caterpillar, one I'd like to squash.

Without asking, Gorski walks past me. His gaze travels around my apartment, taking in my recent changes. A new secondhand couch to replace the one Tory stained, a new lamp and side table—thanks to the Humane Society. Not to mention the paint job. His eyes land on the chest freezer, but I doubt he's guessed its true identity, disguised with a tablecloth and candles.

"We've got a few follow-up questions, Mrs. Bardo."

I nod.

"New furniture?"

"Secondhand."

"What happened to the old stuff?"

"Don't know. I left it by the dumpster."

That's a lie. Habitat for Humanity came by and picked it up.

"You met with the insurance adjuster, Tory Hartmann?"

"Yeah." My eyes dart to Redbear, the ballpoint racing on his pad. What if he's not really a police officer? What if he's an operative of CORN? I choose my words carefully. "I thought she was satisfied with my answers and the case was closed."

"It appears that way," Gorski says.

"What do you mean, *appears*?"

"I mean, it appears that way according to a text she sent to her home office."

"Isn't that good enough?"

"Usually, in cases like this, there's paperwork, forms filled out and filed, but due to the demise of Ms. Hartmann—"

"Demise?"

"Her death." Gorski's eyes bore into me.

The Xanax is kicking in, so my knee's stopped shaking, but I feel like I'm underwater. The world around me ripples like a mirage—Gorski and Redbear, the new couch, the pictures on the wall, the pattern on the tablecloth. My face prickles with cold sweat. I know I'm breathing, my heart is pumping, but I feel disconnected from my body.

Redbear looks up from his pad.

Definitely an operative.

"You didn't know Ms. Hartmann died? Been all over the news."

"I don't have cable."

They both stare at me as if I'm screwy, glance at my Smart TV.

"I stream."

Redbear scribbles frantically, and Gorski stares at me until I break the silence.

"I didn't know she died," I say. Then, thanks to all the true crime shows I've watched, I remember to sound concerned and ask, "When? How?"

"Car accident," Gorski says. "Shortly after she spoke to you."

My vision is breaking up, flashes of light shattering Gorski's face so his mouth is where his nose should be. My synapses fire randomly, shooting sparks.

Condition red.

"Car drove off a cliff." Redbear looks up from his pad. "You didn't know that?"

I shake my head, my brain going haywire.

Condition red, condition red, red, red.

Gorski says, "Tell us about your meeting."

My system is shutting down. New data is available, but I can't download the information. My stomach feels queasy. I might have picked up a virus.

"Too much spam."

"What?"

My head snaps toward Gorski.

"What's this about Spam?" he asks.

"She ate too much," I say.

Nice save!

"I gave her Spam and crackers, and she drank several glasses of wine. I didn't realize she intended to drive to Denver."

Gorski glances at Redbear. "The autopsy mention Spam?"

"Don't think so." Redbear cocks his head. "How'd you know she was headed to Denver?"

My mind is blank, my hard drive wiped.

"I, ah—" I'm scrambling for backup. "I assumed. I mean, she mentioned she came from Denver, and when you said her car went off a cliff, I figured she must have been heading north."

Shut up! Shut up! Shut up!

I lick my lips.

Wonder if I should call a lawyer—at least upgrade my Norton. I need a better firewall.

"You stated she drank wine," Gorski says. "That's been confirmed by the autopsy. Did she take any pills in your presence?"

"I—maybe. Why?"

"It seems strange that a person would take sleeping pills before a long drive."

"Sleeping pills?" They know about the Unisom. I wonder if they noticed it last time they came here—I remember Redbear sneaking around. "Now that you mention it, she took some kind of pills out of her briefcase. I thought she was taking vitamins or something."

"Her briefcase survived the fire," Redbear says, his face a placid mask. "No bottle."

"Huh."

His eyes glare at me, attempting to locate information, but he needs a better search engine.

"May I use your bathroom, Mrs. Bardo?"

"Uh—yeah."

He hits the bathroom down the hall. I'm worried, not because he'll find evidence—I've scrubbed and bleached the tub, floor tiles, walls, ceiling, and despite a few sanguineous episodes, the bathroom is spotless—but he may bug the place for CORN. No doubt Corporate Operatives Reordering Neuropathy would like nothing better than to thwart me. On the other hand, if he's really just a cop, and he's looking for Unisom, he'll find a brand new, unopened box of SleepGels in the bathroom off my bedroom. Tory polished off the last bottle.

From the corner of my eye, I see Redbear slip down the hall, enter my bedroom. Good thing I got rid of the old chainsaw. He'll find the new one in the closet—no law against that—and if he checks out the bathroom cabinet, he'll find Motrin, Xanax, store brand Pepto Bismol (sometimes I get indigestion); no open Unisom.

While Redbear snoops around my bathrooms, Gorski checks out my kitchen.

"Smells good," he says, eyeing the pot on the stove.

"Ragoût."

"Ragoo? What's that?"

"A kind of stew. I like to cook."

He removes the lid and steam rises from the pot. Between a Shitake and a Morel, I notice an eyeball. I slam the lid down.

"It's not good to let the heat escape. Makes the meat tough."

"I'm lucky if my wife makes Hamburger Helper."

"Sometime I'll invite you for dinner."

Redbear returns with the box of Unisom.

"Same stuff?" Gorski asks.

"Yeah, but this is unopened."

"I have trouble sleeping. The pharmacist at the supermarket recommended I try that stuff, but I'm not big on pills. Is that what Ms. Hartmann took?"

"Not big on pills, but you take Xanax?" Redbear produces a prescription vial.

"The shrink I saw after the rape prescribed it." My tone is sharp. "You guys have a search warrant?"

"She's right," Gorski says to Redbear. "Put those pills back where you found them."

"But forensics says—"

"Put them back. Why use Unisom to drug someone if you have Xanax? One little pill mixed with alcohol is enough to knock out a grown man, let alone a smallish woman."

Good point.

And one that I'll remember.

Redbear hands me the vial of Xanax and the doorbell rings.

"My company."

"We'll be on our way," Gorski says.

"Next time, bring a warrant."

"I doubt there'll be a next time, Mrs. Bardo. Sorry to trouble you."

"WHAT DID THEY WANT?" MARCUS asks me.

"Nothing."

"The cops stopped by for no reason?"

"Forget them." I plant myself in front of Marcus and unzip the jumpsuit, exposing cleavage. "Like my outfit?"

His gaze travels down.

"Bit early for Halloween."

That's not the response I want.

"Do you think I'm sexy?"

I jerk my chin, attempting to toss strands of Tory's red tresses provocatively, but the hairpins come undone and the scalp slips.

"What the hell is that?" Marcus asks. "A dead squirrel?"

This is *not* going according to plan.

"Want some wine?"

"Sure."

Still upset about the dead squirrel comment, I stomp to the kitchen and he follows me.

He picks up the wine bottle, examines the label. "Australian, nice."

"Sit down." I wave him toward the couch.

While Marcus digs into the snacks I've set on the side table—my updated version of pork rinds: couch potato skins—I prepare his wine. Acting on Gorski's suggestion, I'm dousing the Shiraz with Xanax. It's a tougher process than squeezing out a gelcap. I have to crush the pills into powder. I turn my back to Marcus, so he can't see what I'm doing.

Glancing over my shoulder, I see he's happily munching on the skins.

I stir a spoon around the glass, encouraging the white powder to dissolve.

"Have you spoken to your daughter lately?"

"Carmela's doing great, excited about school. I spoke to her this morning."

"What grade's she in?"

"Second. How's your dad?"

"Better. He bought a pair of sandals."

"Sandals?"

"On sale at Zappos. His first attempt at online shopping."

I approach Marcus with his glass of wine, a fake smile glued onto my face.

"Cheers."

I clink his glass with mine.

"Thanks, Sadie."

Perching on the arm of the couch, I take a sip and Marcus takes a gulp. In the background, Frank serenades us.

"How's the wine?"

"A little bitter."

"Grease takes the edge off." I offer him the plate of skin.

"What's this song?"

"Just in Time."

"I wouldn't guess you to be a fan of Tony Bennett."

"Sinatra. I can be sentimental."

"Really?"

"Corny as Kansas in August—or Olathe, as the case may be." I smile at him, but I don't think he gets my reference. Nodding at his glass, I say, "Drink up."

He does as he's told.

"Hungry?"

"Starved."

"Me too."

I take his empty glass, head to the kitchen to refill it.

"Just a few finishing touches on dinner. You like ragoût?"

"Don't know if I've ever had it, but it smells delicious."

I hand him another glass of wine, rev the music's volume, "If Ever I Would Leave You," and go back to the kitchen to bang around some pots and pans.

I call out to Marcus, "Do you believe in soul mates?"

"Soul makes?" He chuckles, then repeats himself, enunciating, "SOUL MATES."

"You laughing at me?"

"Laughing at myself." His voice sounds sort of heavy. "This wine is getting to me. I need to eat."

"Dinner's almost ready. Answer my question."

"What question?"

"Do you believe in soul mates? Two people who complete each other."

"That's called codependence, Sadie."

"You're not very romantic, are you?"

"I'm a realist."

"Me too."

I ladle ragoût into a bowl, grate cheese over it and find a spoon. Xanax acts faster than Unisom. When I return to the couch and try to hand the bowl to Marcus, his head droops toward his chest. I set the bowl on the side table, remove the empty wineglass from his hand.

"Hard day at the office?"

"Yeah." He yawns.

"Screw any of your patients lately?"

"What?"

"Like you screwed me."

"What are you talking about, Sadie? There a problem with your bill?"

He stares at me with drug-glazed eyes.

"Don't pretend you don't remember."

"Remember what?"

"Our session."

"You mean, do I remember how you attempted to seduce me? How I had to fight you off?"

"You raped me. Fucked me on the floor."

"Are you delirious?"

"No worries. I don't plan to report you."

"Sadie, you're delusional."

"Am I? You almost bit my nipple off." To prove it, I unzip my jumpsuit to my navel, revealing my bruised boob.

"What is that? Purple eye shadow? I knew I shouldn't come here."

Marcus wobbles when he stands, and I rush to support him. His aftershave creeps into my nostrils and I feel my body juicing up. He leans on me, thinks we're headed to the front door, but I lead him to the freezer masquerading as a table. I need a flat surface, preferably elevated.

I blow out the candles, push the candlesticks aside, and shove Marcus onto the tablecloth.

"Lie down."

He's too out of it to resist as I pull off his pants. When he speaks his words are slurred.

"What're you doing?"

"Giving you a BJ you'll never forget."

"You're insane."

"Borderline."

"Revising my dio-dio-nosis," he says, groggily. "Anti-Social Personality Disorder. Whadya puddin that wine?"

"Xanax. Only the best for my soul mate."

"How much?"

"Four tablets altogether."

"Exa-exa-exasss-cerbated by alcohol," Marcus mutters, his head lolling from side-to-side. "You trying to kill me?"

"The opposite," I say, although I doubt he hears me. "I want to keep you alive."

He's out. Lying faceup on the freezer. It's almost the perfect length for his body—a bit short for a coffin though (in case I change my mind).

I pour myself another glass of wine. Turn up the music. Take in the scene.

That's when I realize my mistake.

Marcus, supine on what appears to be a table in the middle of my dining area, is visible to anyone who walks into the apartment. The super. The police. My father (not that he'd show up). What was I thinking? I should have bought a freezer with wheels, so I could roll him into the spare room down the hall. Not only that, how can I store anything inside the freezer while he's lying on top of it?

I stare at him, my annoyance growing.

He's off center. The lack of symmetry vexes me. Wedging my hands under his shoulder blades and buttocks, I attempt to roll him onto his stomach, but deadweight is difficult to move. To gain more leverage, I climb onto the freezer. Channeling Natalia Romanova, I maneuver him into a prone position, his face smushed into the wrinkled tablecloth.

Now he's centered, but his feet are not aligned with the edge of the freezer.

Maybe if I remove his shoes.

I untie his Asics Gel-Excels (for once, he's dressed casually) and slip them from his feet. His toes still overreach the freezer, and there's a teeny hole in the bottom of his left sock.

Irritating.

I pull off one sock, then the other, maintaining symmetry. Stare at his naked toes.

They're dangling off the freezer. Usually, at this point, I'm feeling something: excitement, elation, ecstasy ... at least titillation. But, staring at Marcus and his mismatched toes, I feel exasperated.

I fetch my trusty scissors from the kitchen drawer.

Snip.

The little toe is gone, no problem.

Marcus moans, but he's so out of it, he hardly moves. Not enough to stimulate my libido. I thought it would be different for us, thought by now he'd have a hard-on—at the very least I'd have a clit-on. Doctor Phil says a good sexual relationship is one that's gratifying to both partners. I'm disappointed to learn, when it comes to Marcus, no matter how much I lust after his brain, our sex drives may be disparate.

Snip, snip, snip.

Four toes down, and still no movement.

His member peeks between his thighs, limp as shelled escargot, but his foot spouts more blood than I expected. That's a turn-on. It's spurting all over my jumpsuit, soaking through the tablecloth, dripping off the freezer, and ruining the carpet.

Darn.

I run to the hall closet and find my duck tape. (I looked it up online, and *duck* is acceptable—especially with orange sauce.) I tear off a strip and wrap it around his foot to stop the bleeding. Then I pull off a longer strip and tape Marcus to the freezer. For good measure, I slap a slab over his mouth; if he wakes up, I don't want him to upset my neighbors.

Snip, snip, snip.

A few more toes, and I feel concupiscent. In other words, I'm horny. Familiar heat courses through my body, hitting all my pleasure centers. Using his big toe as a dildo, I stimulate my clit. Meanwhile, I pop a smaller toe into my mouth, roll it over my tongue savoring the flavor. It's about the size of grape. The texture would be tenderer without a bone. And yet, the bone lends substance, gives me something to suck on.

Do midgets have small penises?

I think not.

Tyrion Lannister in *Game of Thrones* is quite the swordsman. The thought of well-endowed midgets—or to be politically correct, people little in all ways, but one—really gets me going. Falling to the floor, I roll around, humping myself with the toe. Screeching like a hyena, writhing like a nest of cobras, exploding like a volcano; my neighbors must think I'm Discovery Channel's biggest fan.

Or maybe HBO, since as I come, I scream, "Tyrion!"

Emerging from an orgiastic haze, my focus returns to Marcus.

Overall, I'm delighted with the result of the pedicure I've given him. His feet are now in line with the edge of the freezer. Humming along with Sinatra, I bind the bleeding stumps with tape.

His eyes fly open. He stares at me with disbelief, tries to scream, but duck tape mutes the sound. Wide awake now, despite Xanax and wine, he thrashes around and comes close to falling off the freezer as he attempts to extricate himself.

"Calm down!"

I run into the kitchen, snatch a cast iron pan off the stove, and slam his head.

That shuts him up.

Frank belts, "I Did It My Way," and I sing along.

HEART

THE GOOD THING ABOUT WORK is it takes my mind off things I don't want to think about.

Things like Marcus stinking up my condo.

Thanks to a dolly I borrowed from the supermarket, I moved the freezer to the spare room. On my way there, I dropped Marcus in the bathtub. I think he's pretty comfortable. I gave him a pillow, several cushions I don't care about, and an old blanket. Plus I don't need to worry if he messes himself when there's easy access to water and a drain. He ruined the carpet in the dining area. I pulled it out and dragged the bloody thing downstairs—no help from him. These days he's pretty useless. When the super saw the carpet in the dumpster, she scolded me, said it would attract bears. She was right. They tore it to shreds.

Bears are everywhere this summer.

Even in the break room.

The *Gazette* is always strewn across the table, half-buried under donut boxes and the remains of sandwiches. One day the front page screams: **Bear Attack!** I take in the headline, but I don't read the article, because it pisses me off. From gossip I hear around the store, I know the article mentions two senior citizens, residents of Happy Valley, who lost their lives along the bike path—presumed victims of a bear, since their bodies were gored beyond recognition. If not for dental records, they would not have been identified. Officials recommend carrying pepper spray.

Today the *Gazette* totes another headline: **Lost in Wilderness?** I read that article, and it made me madder than the old folks' story. According to the paper, a tourist, a local actor, and some woman I once met, have been reported missing. They set out on a backpacking trek along the Colorado Trail and never reached their destination. Search parties have discovered nothing, and the three hikers are suspected to be dead. "Probably veered off the trail," the sheriff says. "Ten miles up dogs lost the scent due to recent snowfall in the high country." Conclusion: the hikers are presumed dead due to exposure. The bodies may be buried under snow, or they may have been consumed by bears.

That's bullshit. Bear shit, to be exact.

In Colorado, we have Black Bears—that's a species, not a color. Black Bears can be brown, reddish, or honey-blonde. They're not naturally aggressive; they're mostly vegetarian and rarely attack humans, unless you interfere with their food supply. Sometimes they become habituated to humans, and then they can be dangerous. Not because they want to eat you, but because you're blocking them from dinner. A dumpster. Your refrigerator. The pot roast in your slow cooker. Generally, bears prefer berries to humans.

If authorities want to know what happened to those people in the newspaper, they should speak to me. I pull out my cell, and I'm on the verge of dialing 911 and confessing, when I think of Marcus.

He needs me.

And I need him.

We've taken our relationship to a new level, beyond sex, practicing nonviolent communication and making sure both of our needs are met. If I report myself to the police, that will be the end of me and Marcus. All our hard work will be for naught. I decide to take the high road; I will not allow my ego, an infantile desire for notoriety, to screw up our relationship. Commending myself on the strides I've made recently, when it comes to personal growth, I slip the phone back into my pocket.

I've been reading *The Power of Now*, and it's helped me become more selfless. That's self*less*, not *ish*. There's a world of difference.

For example, instead of thinking only of myself, *my* needs, *my* appetites, I've been thinking about Marcus. I've become more generous—spending my spare time with him, cooking special meals, feeding him large doses of Xanax (I had him write me a prescription for maximum strength), so he doesn't feel much pain. Now and then, I allow the drugs to wear off. When he's lucid, we have great conversations about important topics: life, death, psychology. I asked him to explain the difference between a sociopath and psychopath. He said, no matter how you slice it, *that's* what I am.

I can't blame him for being grouchy. He has health problems. He's lost a lot of blood, and he may have an infection, but his brain is in great shape. I adore his brain, love the way he thinks, and I wonder if it might be possible to keep his head alive without his body. Stephen Hawking claims a brain's programming could live forever if it's stored on a computer. Great minds think alike, I guess. I just need to figure out how to upload Marcus's brain onto my iPhone, so I can carry him in my pocket. Better yet, I'd like to load the contents of his brain directly into mine. I may need a few more megabytes.

This work is all-consuming.

Yesterday I visited the science museum where a kid—six years old, or maybe seven—gave a lecture on robotics. After the lecture, I approached the kid and asked him a few questions. I mentioned the challenge I'm facing regarding programming and uploading information. The kid offered to help me design a robot (he's built several) but he needs to do more research on his dog before attempting to transfer human brain data.

I can't wait to walk around with Marcus's mind inside my brain. How cool will that be? Marcus is more analytical than I am, and his brain will be useful when it comes to planning events, but after speaking to the science kid I doubt the transfer will happen by Labor Day.

Sometimes I think I should feel guilty.

Isn't there a law protecting intellectual property?

Then I tell myself thoughts belong to everyone. Any thought that anyone has ever had is available through the collective unconscious. According to Eckhart Tolle, we're all One. He says, underneath the illusion of separate physical forms, we're all connected—an intricate network of subsystems specializing in specific functions, ultimately controlled and unified by an infinite motherboard. Ideas float around, and if we snatch one, finders keepers.

The problem is keeping Marcus alive until technology catches up with me. Quadriplegics survive, even with no arms or legs. As long as I keep Marcus's head connected to his torso, I think he'll be fine, but once that tie has been severed, I need to find a way to pump blood to his brain.

The intercom breaks into my thoughts.

"Customer Service wanted at the Salad Bar."

Customer Service means me.

No doubt we've run out of lettuce or salad bowls. I hurry from the break room, preparing to placate an angry customer, beeline past the check stands and head to Produce.

One week till Labor Day and the Grand Opening. Produce looks upscale enough to rival Whole Foods or Trader Joe's. They reorganized the vegetable and fruit bins, replaced the scuffed linoleum tile floor with simulated wood, revamped the Salad Bar, and the wet rack is spectacular. Little kids adore the thunderstorm effect.

Cautiously, I approach the Salad Bar. Instead of finding an irate customer, I spot Krista peering through the sneeze guard at a bin of spinach. I head toward the onion display and hope she hasn't noticed me.

"Sadie!"

"Oh-uh, Krista. Hi. How're you?"

"Why haven't you answered my texts?"

"I-uh, I've been busy."

"Doing what?"

"You know, working, projects—"

"Sculpting?"

"You could say that."

I think of Marcus, or what's left of him, lying in my bathtub. The rest of him—toes tucked away in Tupperware, calves wrapped in butcher paper, right thigh encased with heavy-duty aluminum foil to avoid freezer burn—is safely stored inside my *Kenmore Elite*. Arms, hands, most of the left thigh, are still intact. As is his penis—although, these days, that organ has proved sadly disappointing. I plan to harvest the remainder of his left thigh, so I can make a Christmas roast encrusted with rosemary and garlic ... served with a tangy orange sauce or tart cherries or traditional horseradish and sour cream. Which do you think would be yummier? Like all good cooks, I prefer fresh meat to frozen. But I doubt Marcus will make it to the holidays.

I hate spending Christmas alone, and no way am I visiting my father. Not after last year's fiasco. But first I need to survive this summer, not to mention Krista's current interrogation.

"You never showed for anatomy class."

"Yeah, I know." I shift from foot to foot, mapping out my best escape route.

"How can you sculpt if you don't understand anatomy?"

"I'm working on it."

Cocking her head, she studies me.

"You look different, Sadie."

"Do I?"

"You ever go for counseling?"

"I'm seeing a psychiatrist."

Big mistake. Krista knows everyone.

"Who are you seeing?"

"Marcus," his name blasts out of my mouth, before I stop myself.

"Archuleta?"

"Yeah."

"I heard he left town unexpectedly."

"Really?"

"His receptionist and I take the same yoga class— Kundalini, Monday evenings, you should try it—she told me Dr. Archuleta stopped showing at the office. No explanation. Just a voice mail."

I don't mention this to Krista, but, actually, I made that call. A damned good impersonation, IMO.

"She said Marcus sounded weird, not like himself at all. When did you last see him, Sadie?"

"A while ago."

"You okay?"

"Yeah. I'm great."

Krista's eyes meet mine, and I see her concern.

My left eye twitches.

"If you want help, Sadie, I know people—"

"Help with what?"

"Post-Traumatic Stress Disorder, or whatever ..."

Whatever hangs between us like a big, fat question mark.

My left eye is going bonkers, twitching and tearing. I'm sure Krista notices.

I focus on the Salad Bar, say, "I'd better get more lettuce."

Before Krista can stop me, I charge through Deli, hit Bakery, and head for the freight elevator. Safe inside the employee-only zone, I pause to catch my breath. My heart slams into my chest, like it's committing suicide.

I punch the button, summoning the elevator.

Punch it three more times.

There's perspiration on my forehead, but I'm not warm, I'm shivering.

I need a Xanax, fast.

Finding the vial in the pocket of my apron (I keep it with me at all times), I force myself to swallow a pill without the benefit of water. It lodges in my throat, and I try to cough it up.

The elevator door slides open, and I'm still coughing.

"You okay, Sadie?"

Trying not to choke, I nod at the Store Manager. Since my interview with him, at least he knows my name, or maybe he just read my nametag.

"Sure you're okay?"

He eyeballs my heaving chest.

I make a guttural, piggy sound, attempting to dislodge the pill.

"Have a great day, Sadie."

A loud hiccup escapes my mouth.

Maintaining a wide berth, the Store Manager steps out of the elevator as I enter.

My next hiccup is a screech.

Mercifully, the door closes.

On the ride down, my throat continues to convulse, making noises like the neighbor's cat trying to dislodge a hairball. (Of course it doesn't do that now.) When the elevator reaches the basement, I exit in a hurry, in case the security guy caught my coughing fit on camera; I've heard he plays back funny clips for all his friends. Still hiccupping, I walk past the compactor, in search of the dried fruit and nut cart, and hit a construction zone. Planks of wood and strips of aluminum are stacked along the hallway. A large box containing a display case stands beside metal double doors that are usually locked. Today someone left the doors ajar.

"Hello?"

My voice echoes through the cavernous room. So do my hiccups.

The double doors lead to an area beneath the store's showroom, the supermarket's inner sanctum. My sneakers are silent as I tread across the concrete floor. A hum pervades the space, generated by some unknown source of power. Lured by the hypnotic sound, I move deeper into the adytum. The hum becomes louder, pulses through me.

My forehead smacks something cold and hard. A maze of PVC, steel, cast iron, and copper pipes crisscross the ceiling. Some hang so low I have to duck under them—tubing to feed refrigeration, gas lines for ovens, pressurized water for kitchens and bathrooms. On the far wall a mishmash of colored wires creeps over the concrete, supplying electricity to fluorescent overheads and display lights, cash registers, intercom, air-conditioning, and (for all I know) an electric chair for wayward employees.

Standing in the heart of the building, I listen to the thrum.

An electric pulse, feeding juice to the store's internal organs.

Symbolic, don't you think?

Cardboard boxes—some empty, some filled with equipment—are strewn across the floor. My gaze travels to a carton marked: **PUMPS.** The flaps of the box are torn, allowing me to peer inside. Pumps for the sprinkler system.

I extract a coronary artery.

Recipe:
Sadie's Kraut and Knuckles

You don't need a German to make this recipe; any nationality will do. I'm using Marcus, and I believe his heritage is Mexican, or maybe Spanish. In any case, Archuleta County is named after his family. The point is: use whatever knuckles you have on hand (or foot), even pig will do. This is a great dish to make in autumn, when evenings are chilly.

Kraut and Knuckles

Ingredients:

2 pounds knuckles, fresh or smoked
Salt (for fresh knuckles—use salt sparingly; too much is bad for your health)
Ground black pepper
1 teaspoon caraway seeds
1 clove garlic, minced
¼ to ½ cup unsalted butter
1 onion, finely chopped
2 apples, coarsely chopped
½ cup dried mushrooms
Juniper berries—I get these bluish berries from a

Juniper tree down in the courtyard
1 package sauerkraut, 26 oz.

1 cup amber ale
2 cups broth (see Sadie's Basic Soup Stock recipe)

Preparation:

Score the skin of the knuckles. Combine salt, garlic, and caraway seeds in a bowl. (Omit salt if you're using smoked knuckles.) Rub the knuckles with the garlic and caraway combination, making sure the mixture penetrates the scored skin. Melt butter in a skillet. Brown meat and remove.

Rinse sauerkraut. Add more butter to the skillet. Sauté chopped onions on medium heat until golden, add sauerkraut, apples, mushrooms, a few Juniper berries, ale. Bring to a boil. Place the knuckles on top of the kraut and lower heat. Add broth and cover. Cook for 1—1.5 hours, until meat and kraut are tender. Add water or stock as it cooks, if necessary. When done, remove the knuckles and cut meat from the bones. Place sauerkraut on a platter with meat on top. Serve with rye bread.

MENTAL HEALTH

WHEN I GET HOME FROM work, first thing, I run to the bathroom to see Marcus.

I changed the doorknob, so it locks from the outside now. Not that Marcus can climb out of the tub. Lack of feet would make that difficult, but his right leg is completely gone, so walking is impossible. I've removed his left leg to the knee, but he still has both arms. I suppose he could hoist himself out of the tub and, if he managed to escape the bathroom, he might *drag* himself across the living room (unless he's taught himself to hop on the stump of his remaining thigh). Then he might open the front door and slide (or roll) down the stairway to the courtyard.

I fiddle with the bathroom lock, afraid of what I'll find. Even though I've loaded him with Xanax, lately his mood has been foul.

My fears are unfounded.

He's in the tub, asleep.

Actually, he may have drifted into coma.

Having reassured myself that Marcus is safe and sound, I head to the kitchen to make a soothing cup of Kava tea. It's late, almost time for bed, and I don't want to risk caffeine. Kava-Kava is a plant popular throughout the Pacific islands, including Hawaii, Polynesia and Melanesia. When steeped, the roots of Kava-Kava produce a sedative effect which I find relaxing.

I need to relax. Lately, despite increased dosages of Xanax, my nerves have been on edge.

While my tea brews, I untangle the rubber tubing of the pump I confiscated from the supermarket, then I return to the bathroom and plug the pump into an outlet. The motor whirs, so the thing works, but I need to figure out how to hook it up to Marcus. I don't want to wake him, so I fill the sink with water (I need to find a source of blood), stick the tubing in his ear, and rev the motor to high speed. The water spurts with so much force I may have ruptured his eardrum.

His eyelids open, and he stares at me like I'm some kind of monster.

The damned pump spews water all over the bathroom, all over me. I manage to turn it off, but not before my socks are soaked. The wool clings to my toes, and my feet feel like they're suffocating.

I sound like my father.

The horror of this realization sends me into a downward spiral. If I'm turning into my father, what hope do I have for the future? Cans of store brand soup and burnt white toast, hours watching *Jeopardy* without knowing any answers, cataracts and thinning hair?

I glance at the mirror to check if I've gone bald. I need another dye job, my roots are showing.

At times like this, it's important to *think positive.*

Sitting on the toilet, I pull the wet socks from my feet, toss them on the floor.

Marcus makes an annoying wheezing sound.

In an effort to improve his breathing, I rip the duck tape from his mouth.

Truthfully, he doesn't look good. He's lost a lot of muscle and his hair's gone grayer—even the hair on his chest. The Saint Christopher medal he refuses to take off sits in a scraggly nest of gray. I'm not sure what I ever saw in him. His complexion is the color of toothpaste, greenish-blue. The whites of his eyes are bloodshot, the corners crusted with yellow stuff. His lips are crusty too, and it takes a lot of effort for him to move them. The grimace he offers me is not attractive.

"Would you like some Kava tea, Marcus?"

I have to lean close to hear him.

"Fuck you."

He says fuck a lot. I never realized how much he cursed, until he moved in. It's amazing what you learn about another person when you live in close proximity.

"Have some tea. It will relax you."

"Fuck you, you fucking psycho."

"Is that your professional diagnosis?"

"Fuck, yes."

"I don't think that's how a psychiatrist should speak."

"Go to hell."

"Would you like some sauerkraut? It's homemade."

He tries to sit, but with one stump, he has trouble gaining traction and slips to the bottom of the tub. I reach behind his head, attempting to rearrange his cushions, but he slaps my hand away.

"Marcus, I'm trying to help you."

"Just kill me, bitch."

"No need for nasty names."

I pull away his blanket, revealing what remains of his left leg. I wrapped his stump with duck tape to stop the bleeding, but it's leaking greenish pus. Nothing much remains of his right leg, just a ragged bit of thigh. It looks red and swollen. The duck tape bandages make it impossible for me to tell if his stumps are healing.

I poke his knee, checking for infection.

He grabs my wrist and bites.

"Oooowwww!"

He sinks his teeth deeper, breaking the skin.

I jerk my hand away.

"Animal!"

Holding up my wounded hand, I watch blood ooze from my wrist and trickle down my arm. *My blood.* It's staining my uniform. *I don't deserve this kind of treatment.* I'm trying to control my temper, but there's only so much I can take.

I run my tongue over my teeth, feeling the sharp points of my canines.

He's thrashing his arms, trying to escape, attempting to stand on his stump, but he keeps falling.

I remind myself not to yell, to practice nonviolent communication, but how can I feel empathy for a person who bites me like a rabid animal?

"Kill me, Sadie, please. Get it over with."

"No."

"Why not?"

"I don't want to spend the holidays alone."

"Labor Day?"

"There's also Columbus Day, Veteran's Day, Halloween, Thanksgiving and *Christmas*." I emphasize Christmas, because it's a sore point.

"You have your dad."

I snort.

Last year, when I visited my father, he insisted we go Christmas shopping, so I took him to the mall. Macy's. I parked the car, we got as far as *Shoes*, and then he took off, shooting through the store at about fifty miles per hour. Spotting his orange *Suns'* cap bobbing through the crowd, I attempted to follow him. In case you've never been there, Macy's is a madhouse during the holidays. I lost him around *Men's Wear*. Had to call Security.

We found him fingering the panties in *Women's Lingerie*.

Marcus *knows* this story, knows the trauma it caused me.

"I'm sending socks for Christmas."

Marcus groans.

"I'm not going to see my father. I'd rather shoot myself than spend another holiday with him."

"I'll lend you a gun."

I bare my teeth at Marcus, growl.

"The holidays are meant for family," he says, sadly.

I know he's thinking of his daughter.

"You miss Caramel?"

His lower lips trembles. It's kind of gross to see a grown man cry, and Marcus is blubbering.

Really, I have no idea why I used to find him appealing.

"If you're good, I may let you call your daughter—"

"Please—"

"Just don't bring up Daddy again."

After locating him in *Lingerie*, I dragged my father down the escalator and out of Macy's. That's when the alarms went off. He'd stuffed the pockets of his jacket with several Miracle Bras, four animal print thongs (zebra, leopard, tiger, and giraffe), a chartreuse garter belt, red satin chemise, and pink Baby Doll pajamas. He returned his treasures and, thankfully, Security didn't press charges. But I didn't discover the teddy (black lace, crotchless, size 4X) until we got back to his place. He wore it underneath his flannel shirt and corduroys, refusing to take it off even when he showered.

Recalling that nightmare, I let out a long sigh.

And then I sniff.

Marcus messed himself again. Adult diapers may in order (my dad uses those), but how will they stay put with just one stump?

"Want a bath, Marcus?"

He doesn't answer.

He appears to be unconscious.

Shaking his shoulder has no effect.

Neither does nibbling his earlobe. It's so tender, my canines slide right through the flesh.

Pump or no pump, he won't make it past Labor Day.

No Marcus for the holidays.

I know I should feel *sad*. I recognize the word, can even mimic the behavior. Rubbing my eyes, I make a sobbing sound and manage to squeeze out a few tears. But I can't fathom how sad *feels*.

Maybe that's a good thing.

Is *not* being sad the same as being happy? If happy is the antithesis of sad, I *must* be elated. According to the self-help books I've read, happiness is a sign of enlightenment. I don't feel a smidge of sorrow, so I guess I'm pretty evolved. I used to call myself Sad Sadie, but lately my outlook has become cheerful. I attribute this amazing transformation not only to positive *thinking*, but positive *action*. I want to reiterate this point: Wishing for change won't make change happen. You have to *be* the change and change your *actions*. Don't fall into the trap of magical thinking.

Like Marcus.

He's definitely on his last leg—also his last arm. Gangrene has set it. I checked it out online at the Mayo Clinic's site, and in the state of his condition, surgery is the only alternative, so I hack off his right arm.

He really thinks I'm going to let him call his daughter?

GRAND OPENING

WORK, *WORK, WORK, WORK, WORK, work, work.*
Last night is a blur. I didn't sleep, and now I'm going to be late.

I pedal my bike faster, hoping to avoid impending rain. The weather report calls for thunderstorms all weekend. Dark clouds cloak the mountains, and I already felt a sprinkle. Riding my bike may have been a mistake. I consider turning back to get my late husband's truck. (The thing still starts. I used it recently to haul a load.) But, due to the Grand Opening tomorrow, a refrigerated trailer of meat is parked in back of the supermarket and there's no room for employee vehicles.

The rain becomes a deluge as I reach the parking lot.

I secure my bike on the new rack—really it's the old rack painted green—and run inside the store. Dripping wet, my hair frizzed out like a clown, I head for the time clock. The cashiers appear more stressed than usual; CRMs hover around the front end, like hawks suffering from Attention Deficit Disorder. Courtesy Clerks scurry past—wiping down

Self-Checkout, replacing garbage bags, trying to avoid the wrath of Checkers and CRMs.

I wave to Wendy, but she doesn't notice me.

Strangers from Corporate are holding a meeting at the entrance of the break room, so I have to squeeze past them. For days now, they've been huddling around displays, rearranging shelves, giving instructions and confusing everyone. The Store Manager is on the verge of a nervous breakdown. Of course, that's normal.

After clocking in, I head for Produce. My coworkers are hard at it, heads down as they sort through bananas, avocados, lettuce, mangos. The displays have to be perfect: peppers facing the same way, cucumbers in neat rows, garlic stacked into a pyramid. People will be here all night preparing for tomorrow.

I spot the Produce Manager, slip around the Salad Bar attempting to avoid him.

"Sadie!"

"Yes?"

I stop walking, turn toward him. He looks more distraught than usual, and I wonder if he's drunk.

"Your number one priority is labels. Crawl around the bins and make sure no stickers have attached themselves to the new floor."

"Crawl?"

"That's the only way to find them."

"But, if no one can see the labels—"

"No arguments. Your next number one priority is raisins. No holes."

"No holes in raisins. Got it."

"And your number one, number one priority is—"

You guessed it: corn. I need to cut, shuck, wrap twenty cases. Everywhere you look in Produce signs say: Colorado Grown. And Olathe corn is the star of the show.

The war on bugs is serious, and I've tracked the numbing of my hands to pesticides. Through research online, I've discovered that pesticides are a derivative of nerve gas. It doesn't kill bugs, it numbs their tiny brains and wrecks their tiny neurotransmitters. These days, when I shuck corn, I wear heavy rubber gloves and a *Breaking Bad* respirator.

The freight elevator is stuffed with a pallet of dairy, so I'm forced to take the long way downstairs. I head through Bakery, stopping to sample carrot cake, then continue through Meat and Seafood. I slip through the insulated doorway and hurry down the stairway.

The basement hallway is more packed than usual, cookies and candy nearly toppling from the shelves. Across from the Store Manager's office (his door is closed as usual), pallets of soda block the storage cage. Despite the obstacle course, Terri has managed to gain entrance. Her keys dangle from the padlock. She's inside the cage rearranging cartons. She glances at me as I walk past.

"Hi Sadie. Ready for tomorrow?"

"Almost."

Anxious to escape her scrutiny, I hurry toward Produce. When I'm certain she can no longer see me, I thrust my hand into the pocket of my apron to make sure I still have the Trinidad Scorpion pepper spray.

The workroom is crazier than ever—a maze of boxes stacked to the ceiling. A narrow, twisting path leads to my corner, but to reach it I have to risk an avalanche of peaches. At least, back here behind the crates, no one can see me. I'm safe within my fortress of corn, surrounded by a moat of watermelon.

I find an empty spray bottle marked water, dump in the Scorpion pepper spray, and place the bottle on my salad cart. Using my trusty stepstool, I reach a crate of corn and set it on the counter. Then I set the guillotine over the double bagged trash can and set up an RPC to receive cut ears of corn.

Chop, chop, chop.

I feel calm.

Chop, chop, chop.

In control.

Chop, chop, chop.

I imagine tomorrow. I want to make the day memorable for everyone including customers, not just a select few. I plan to go around the store coating samples with the pepper spray. Nothing obvious. Just my little joke. So when customers bite into a chunk of watermelon, a slice of cake, a mini sandwich from the Deli—their mouths will go up in smoke.

Thinking about the reactions, I chop faster.

In high gear, I grab another crate of corn.

My mind goes blank as I keep chopping.

Chop, chop, chop.

Shuck, shuck, shuck.

Wrap, wrap, wrap.

I'm a machine.

In less than an hour, my salad cart is filled with packages of corn.

Maneuvering my loaded cart through the labyrinth of crates isn't easy. I nearly knock over a stack of peaches. The Hulk, Liam's replacement, is working at the crisping sink, and I ram him intentionally.

"Hey! Watch where you're going."

"Sorry."

Sorry, I didn't ram you harder.

He eyes my cart of corn.

"You don't need all that. We took the outside display down. It's raining like a son of a bitch."

"Is it?"

"I'm not done crisping, but I gotta get this stuff on the wet rack." He nods at a cart loaded with plastic bins of lettuce, broccoli, cilantro. "Want to take that up?"

"Can't," I lie. "I'm not finished down here."

Truthfully, I don't feel like doing favors for Liam's replacement.

"Guess I'll go up then." He lays his knife on the stainless steel counter, hangs his rubber apron on a hook and rolls his cart out the door.

I stay in the work area, so he can't see me, listen for the freight elevator to come and go. When the coast is clear, I roll my cart of corn out the door and follow his wet tracks.

I punch the button to summon the elevator.

A crack of thunder penetrates the basement.

The lights flicker, come back on.

The elevator beeps, stuck on the first floor. I punch the button again, but nothing happens. Someone must be up there loading stuff. Or maybe the break in electricity is making it run slow.

Nothing I can do, but wait.

Sneaking my phone from my pocket (the cameras are watching), I check the time. I'm due for a break. I glance at the elevator door. The button is still lit, so it's got power. I give it another punch. Decide to check my messages.

My father phoned. A text from my sister: Call Dad **NOW**. A text from Krista.

The phone makes a weird noise, and a storm warning alert flashes on the screen. Heavy rain. Flash floods. Power outages.

The elevator beeps again.

The squeak means it's moving.

I stare at the door, watching for light to appear through the small window. Within the patch of glass, I see a face.

Not the new guy.

My heart creeps into my throat.

I swallow.

My impulse is to run, but my feet refuse to move. They're rooted to the concrete floor. I stare in disbelief as the elevator's lips slide open and the grill rises. I peer into the gaping mouth.

"Hello, Sadie."

I lick my lips, sickness rising from my throat.

"I-I thought you were—"

"Dead?"

Justus grins at me, his eyes anything but friendly. He's wearing one of those black boots the hospital gives you after surgery. His neck is encircled by a brace, his left arm encased in plaster, an ace bandage wrapped around his right.

My mind whirs, trying to make sense of the impossible. Justus has come back to life. He steps out of the elevator, moves toward me.

I grab the pepper spray from my cart and spritz him in the face.

He lunges at me, hands rushing to his burning eyes.

"I'm gonna kill you, Sadie!"

The bottle drops from my hands and rolls under the pepper cart.

A blast of thunder rocks the building.

The lights flicker and go out.

THE BASEMENT HALLWAY IS SO dark that I can barely see Justus.

I back away from the elevator, my hands moving along the wall, searching for the doorway into Produce.

I hear Justus breathing.

Smell his aftershave, mingled with the spicy scent of Trinidad Scorpion.

"Remember that day, Sadie?"

"Wh-what day?"

"I saw you standing on your balcony."

"So?"

The stink of the trash compactor overpowers his after-shave, so I must be close to Produce.

Justus grabs my wrist.

"I know you threw that rock."

"What rock?"

He squeezes my wrist, bruising my skin, the pressure of his fingers threatening to snap the bones. His breath comes in gasps, moist and hot.

"I can't prove you threw the rock, so I can't have you fired, but I promise to make your life a misery."

Yanking my arm from his grasp, I stumble through the black void of the hallway until I reach Produce. I push, and the doors swing open. Cold air hits me in the face. I trip over an RPC and slam into a counter, wet and slick from crisping.

Clunk.

Clunk, clunk.

The scrape of Justus's boot on concrete follows me, heavy and uneven.

I stand still, afraid to move.

The sound of every movement is obvious in the black quiet. No hum of electricity emanates from the dark overhead lights, no whir of refrigeration comes from the walk-in cooler, just my own breath—ragged as it escapes my mouth.

The doors swing open.

An RPC clatters to the floor.

Clunk.

Clunk, clunk.

The boot makes Justus unstable.

"Where are you, Sadie?"

Clunk, clunk.

"Shit!"

Boxes crash onto the concrete, followed by the cloying scent of smashed peaches.

"Sadie, I want to talk to you."

Fat chance.

My fingers run over the counter seeking the new guy's knife. It skitters out of my reach, clanks into the sink.

"Sadie?"

I slip under the counter, and hide behind a trash can.

Silence.

Then the scrape of Justus's boot as he maneuvers through the labyrinth of boxes and crates.

He must think I'm in my workspace.

The stainless steel counter runs along the wall, all the way to my workstation, offering me a path that bypasses the labyrinth. If I crawl, I bet I can reach the sinks in back before Justus.

Scrambling along the concrete on my knees, water soaks my pants. My palm skids on a slimy piece of rotten fruit, but I keep going, circling the bin of watermelons.

"I'm coming for you, Sadie."

I emerge at my workstation.

Clunk, clunk.

He's behind the watermelons.

Clunk, clunk, clunk.

I propel myself toward the wall where I keep the knives. A machete in each hand, I turn toward the clunk of his boot.

"You're dead meat, Sadie."

"Ditto."

Machetes raised above my head, I rush toward his voice. I can't see a damned thing, but his screams tell me I've hit the mark. The blades slice easily through flesh. Wet splatters me, but I keep swinging. Justus can howl all he wants, curse me out, call me nasty names—no one hears him down here in the dungeon.

Except maybe Terri.

But she's welcome to join the party.

He's afraid now, running as fast as he can with his bad foot.

Clunk, clunk, clunk, clunk, clunk.

Sliding on soaked concrete, I chase him through the labyrinth. Crates crash around us, spilling cucumbers, peppers, peaches, corn. I kick aside a body part, slip on something slick, probably intestines. Fighting to maintain my balance, I skid into a tower of boxes destined for my nut and raisin cart. The tower collapses, showering me with pistachios.

I land on cold concrete.

Luckily, I didn't slit my throat with the machete.

Sitting on the floor, I nurse my bruised knee. I may have torn some cartilage.

Uneven footsteps run along the hallway.

Justus has escaped.

Tears run down my face. I need to blow my nose. My father is right, I'm nothing but a slacker, a loafer.

No you're not.

She's right.

I'm Sadie the Sadist.

Gathering my pride and the machetes, I stumble to my feet. I make my way through what's left of the labyrinth, dragging my machetes through the carnage, pistachios crunching under my sneakers. My knee twinges from the fall, but that won't deter Sadie the Sadist.

A buzz greets me as I exit Produce.

The emergency generator has kicked on, and shadowy light illuminates the hallway. Not enough power for the elevator, barely enough power to see where I'm going.

I head toward the stairway on the far side of the store.

As I limp past the manager's office, a woman's voice calls out my name.

Terri.

I glance at the cage.

She's happy to see me.

And I'm delighted to see her.

"Oh my Gosh, Sadie, were you caught down here in the dark too? Scary, huh? The storm must have knocked out a power line. I'm so glad the lights are back."

"Me too."

I've been waiting for this moment, and I may have missed it in the dark.

"We should get upstairs. See what we can do to help."

"That's where I'm heading."

"What's with the machetes?"

"I was cutting watermelon when the lights went out."

"We sure go through a lot of cut fruit, don't we, Sadie girl?"

Terri turns her back to me, to relock the cage.

Ignoring my wounded knee, I charge her, the twin blades of my machetes threatening to whack off her hands.

The padlock slips from her grasp.

"Sadie, what—"

Before she knows what's happening, I shove her back inside the cage and secure the gate. I don't have time to play with her right now. There's a bigger fish to fry upstairs.

Clawing at the chain-link, she yells, "What are you doing, Sadie?"

"C U Next Tuesday."

"I think you have your dates mixed up, Sadie. Today is Friday. Tomorrow's the Grand Opening and we all need to be here. See you tomorrow, Sadie. Do you hear me?"

Dumb bitch.

She keeps yelling as I walk toward the stairway.

Talk about dumb, I should have cut her tongue out. I knew Terri is a big talker, but I didn't realize how loud she can scream.

Yanking her tongue out with pliers would be fun.

Later.

Right now, I'm on a mission to find Justus.

JUSTICE FOR JUSTUS

THE METAMORPHOSIS OCCURS AS I ascend the stairway. At first, I barely notice. It's more an absence than a feeling. My knee no longer hurts. After climbing a few stairs, the transformation becomes obvious. My legs grow stronger with each step, my knee's cartilage restructuring. Light flashes through my brain, reprogramming synapses, synching me with an intelligence beyond my physical body.

Synching me with Marcus.

Must be a delayed reaction.

I'm not sure how it's possible, but I know it's happening. Why else would I be thinking thoughts like this: *A dissertation regarding abnormal psychology follows a standardized format and attempts to support or confirm a hypothesis based on the investigator's observations and research in the field. In the case of Sadie the Sadist ...*

Did I tell him about her?

I don't think so.

Proof that he's inside my brain.

You are what you eat and I'm becoming Marcus.

He must be fond of carrots. My eyes have become infrared and penetrate the darkness. Objects that were murky silhouettes are now clearly defined. I'm seeing things I've never noticed—amoebas float past my pupils, creatures peer from shadows, beings from other dimensions. My eyes see through the building, penetrate the walls, the beams and insulation, the roof. My vision reaches past storm clouds, the earth's atmosphere, the solar system, far beyond the Milky Way, as my mind taps into cosmic consciousness. Power floods my legs, and I bound up the stairs, my humanoid body supercharged and primed for action.

I emerge into chaos.

Any fears of Terri's screams being detected are quickly annihilated by the riotous cacophony. Hail pellets the roof, ricocheting like bullets, and the fire alarm shrieks at a decibel designed to rupture sanity. Between claps of thunder, I hear phones go off around the store, reporting destroyed roads, emergency conditions, accidents.

I plug earbuds into my cell, then plug my ears, updating my database.

Widespread power outage.
Main Street flooded.
Interstate severely damaged.
Roads obliterated.
People stranded.
Federal disaster.
Death toll unknown.

The death toll is about to accelerate.

Wielding my machetes, I prowl the store's perimeter in search of Justus.

Thanks to the lack of power, the intercom is gagged. No long-forgotten disco tunes, no cute ads for the Floral

Department, no managers summoning employees to the office for interrogation and torture.

Marilyn Manson streams through my phone, providing a killer soundtrack.

Cut, cut, cut.

The generator supplies enough electricity to power cash registers, barely enough juice to light the aisles, and no power for refrigeration. Coworkers rush around the store in search of cardboard to shield the displays and protect cold food. They're ripping boxes off of shipments, pulling cardboard from the baler—too preoccupied to notice me.

Panicked customers hurry through dimly lit aisles, loading carts with milk, eggs, bread, batteries, and candles—praying they will make it home.

I don't suffer stress.

Robots are protected under warranty.

For grins, I pass a machete through a line of cartons, spilling milk onto the floor. People back away in horror.

Fun!

I hit the yogurt, sour cream, cottage cheese.

Cut, cut, cut.

Justus may be hiding, may be in disguise and trying to avoid me. I look for telltale signs: someone limping, a trail of blood, the scent of Trinidad Moruga Scorpions.

Leaving Dairy, I move along Aisle 12, smashing containers of pain killers, breaking bottles of cough syrup. When I reach the endcap, I push over a display of vitamins.

An old man yells at me.

To shut him up, I whack him with a machete.

Cut, cut, cut.

At the front of the store, I tour the checkout stands in search of Justus. People wait in line, their carts loaded.

Wendy waves at me, and I wave back.

I head to Produce.

Spot Justus by the melons.

Amazingly, after our scuffle in the labyrinth, his body seems to be intact.

But when he turns toward me, I see the plaster on his wounded arm is stained with blood. He's holding his other arm against his stomach, attempting to contain the slippery tube of his intestine.

Raising my machetes, I run toward Justus to deliver a double whammy.

Before I reach him, a crack of thunder shakes the building—so loud it sounds like an explosion.

The store goes black.

A woman screams.

So does a man, but I'm not sure if it's Justus.

I swing the machetes, decapitating, slicing, severing.

Heads roll around my feet, gray matter leaking from the skulls. My ASICS are soaked in blood, and the floor is slick with guts.

I hack some more.

The stench becomes overpowering, unbearable, so acrid I'm crying. Tears stream from my eyes as I hack—eviscerating, gouging, slashing.

Somewhere, over by the Salad Bar, a little boy wails for his mother.

Light streams through the dark, as people activate their cellphones' flashlight apps.

Marilyn is screaming.

I hear sirens, someone shouting.

"Stop! Stop! Stop!"

I'm turning in a circle, machetes extended, blades of a vicious fan. The louder Marilyn screams, the faster I spin, accelerating as I approach orgasm—

"Sadie, stop!"

Coitus interruptus.

That's not Marilyn—it's Marcus.

He's not just inside my head; he's invaded my cha cha, my snatch, fish mitten, wookie—I swear, he's pumping me right here in the middle of Produce, pounding me with vegetables.

Of course, that isn't possible.

I left him at home.

A butternut dildo bangs my G-spot.

"I'm coming, Marcus!"

I keep spinning, like a propeller on steroids, my orgasm building. Heat blasts through me as I whirl faster, pulverizing anything, anybody in my path, so dizzy I can barely stand. I'm screaming, wailing, as the Big O engulfs me. Centrifugal force pulls at my core, sending me one way then another, rearranging my cellular structure, increasing the space between molecules, so my body is permeable, invisible, invincible. No longer solid mass, light flows through me. I'm inter-dimensional, existing on multiple planes, omniscient.

"Look out! She's going down!"

"Oh, oh, oh, oh, oh, oh, oooooohhhhh!"

I fall backward, machetes flying from my hands.

My head hits something hard, and the impact nearly knocks me out. I crash onto the floor. Round objects, the size of heads, bombard me, roll around my body. Beams of lights stream over me. Am I in heaven? If I am, they'll throw me out. An orgasmic spasm sends me into convulsions.

"Are you okay, Sadie?"

"Amazing."

Through the front door's glass, I see fire trucks.

I'm lying in a patch of purple cabbages, a banana lodged between my thighs.

A sign flutters to the floor: Avocados 10 for $10.

"A dollar each, that's a good price."

A buzzing sound permeates the store, followed by a flood of light from the overhead fluorescents.

People cheer.

I look around the new wood floor, expecting to see heads, arms, legs, and other body parts. Expecting to see Justus bleeding. Maybe a few penises. Instead I see mutilated watermelons, juice oozing from cracked rinds, bruised squash and cucumbers, smashed tomatoes.

The stink is explained by a toppled bin of onions, crushed by customers scurrying for cover.

"What happened?"

A woman's voice answers.

"People panicked."

"Because of me?"

"Not because of you, silly." Looking up from a pile of desecrated produce, I see Terri. "When the lights went out, a customer crashed his cart into the watermelon bin, then a lady fell into the tomatoes. That caused a chain reaction involving onions and zucchini which ended when you landed in the cabbages."

"Where's Marcus?"

"Marcus who?"

My eyes narrow as I take Terri in.

"How did you escape?"

"Escape what?"

"The cage."

Cocking her head, she studies me. "Stay right here, hon. I'm gonna ask those nice firemen if they have an EMT. You may have a concussion."

I'm thinking about getting up, wondering how I'll get home, when a black boot appears in front of me.

Justus.

Machetes dangle from his hands, juice dripping off the blades. How he can he stand upright with his intestine spilling from his gut? The sucker is strewn over the floor. Did you know the small intestine of a human is about twenty feet long? That's six meters, almost seven yards. Every time Justus moves, the thing drags behind him like a hose. Pus oozes from his blistered face, and his right eyeball hangs from the socket.

I'm trying to remember what I know about zombies. They eat brains, don't they?

"Get up, Sadie. You're not paid to sit around."

I stand slowly, my eyes glued to Justus, or the thing that looks like him. I don't want a zombie munching on my frontal lobe, snacking on my medulla oblongata. Stepping backward, I trip on a cabbage and hop over a length of intestine. Upon closer inspection, I realize the intestine is an unraveled ace bandage. If he's not a zombie, maybe he's a simulacrum that looks and acts like Justus.

This has to be the work of Terri the Terrible.

Once again, she's outdone me. She's discovered how to upload a human brain into a robot. Not a crumby wannabe robot like that imposter in Deli, but a state-of-the-art humanoid.

That's the only logical explanation.

The boot is a nice touch, so is the neck brace. Realistic.

Justus, or the thing that looks like Justus, says, "Get to work, Sadie."

"Your ace bandage is undone."

He glances down, reels in the strip of fabric.

"You'll need a broom and dustpan to clean this up."

"I need an Umarex Tactical Force TF11, CO2, Black Machine Gun."

I stumble out of the store.

A FIRE TRUCK IS PARKED out front. Red lights pulse through hail and rain, shimmer on the wet pavement. A fireman rushes past me. Medics carrying a stretcher disappear into the store. I hurry through the parking lot toward the bike rack, my head bowed against the downpour. My bicycle is soaked. I run the sleeve of my fleece jacket over the seat and handlebars, but it's a hopeless cause.

The ride home sucks. The river overflowed the banks, destroying the road, and the bike path is flooded.

I pedal through a foot of water.

There's a lump on my head, and I feel kind of dizzy. I hate to admit it, but Terri's diagnosis of a concussion may be accurate. Or maybe I'm deranged, looney, out to lunch ... the English language has a lot of words for crazy.

How can Justus not be dead? I know the accident was real. I saw it. The cops *said* it was real, so did that insurance lady. Justus *must* be dead, so how did he show up tonight? People can't *really* come back from the dead, can they? (When I get home I'm gonna Google *zombies*.) Did anybody *tell* me he was dead? Did I read it in the paper? See it on TV? I can't remember. OMG. I think I'm cuckoo, ape shit, nutty as a fruitcake.

But, what if I'm not?

What if I'm as sane as you?

My fleece jacket provides no protection. Rain seeps through the fabric, plastering my shirt to my back. Mud splatters my face, and my mouth is full of grit. Tasting salt, I realize I'm crying.

Sad Sadie has returned.

I pump the pedals harder, angry at the weather, angry with myself.

The gears slip, and I skid into a puddle. Dirty water splashes me as the bike tilts. My sneakers (practically new) sink into mud. Tears and rain run down my face.

I think of Marcus back home, waiting for me.

I need to see him, want to talk with him.

And he needs me.

That thought keeps me going as I push my bike along the path.

MIND GAMES

I F THERE'S ONE THING I'VE learned from all the self-help books I've read it's this: avoid mind games at all costs. You know the games I mean. For women, it's playing hard to get to pique his interest, trading sex for services, giving him the silent treatment when he's done something you don't like. Men play different games. They feign undying love when all they want is sex, make dates at the last minute because Mr. Happy has a hard-on. The worst mind game is what Marcus did to me: stringing me along—eating my food, hanging out, biding his time and wasting mine while he looked for a better situation. I thought we were above games. I believed our relationship was based on mutual trust, honesty and respect. But now I realize Marcus is a master of manipulation.

The bastard has been playing me.

I arrive at my condominium, my clothes soaked to my skin, my bike a muddy mess. Wearily, I climb the stairs, sneakers oozing water with each step. When I reach the landing, I dig the key out of my pocket, slip it into the lock and open the front door.

"Honey, I'm home!"

Of course, there's no answer.

Am I really expecting one?

Shivering, I remove my wet jacket.

The apartment is strangely quiet, except for my footsteps on the floor's exposed WonderBoard. I haven't had the time or money to replace the carpet.

Standing at the picture window, I watch sheets of rain wash through the courtyard, causing lights to flicker on what appears to be a lake, but really it's the lawn. Somewhere, drowned beneath the rush of water, the sandbox where Caramel played is buried.

I cast my X-ray vision around the living room, searching for evidence. No fingerprints. No DNA, other than what would be expected. The dumpster is filled with empty plastic bottles. No law against using bleach.

On my way to the bathroom, I stop in the kitchen and put the kettle on. After the evening's events—the shock of seeing Justus returned from the dead—I need a cup of Kava.

Pausing at the thermostat, I bump up the heat.

My fingers are cold and numb, so I have trouble turning the bolt on the bathroom door. I'm not sure what I expect to find, but I'm imagining a romantic bubble bath for two. Since Marcus is sans legs, we should fit comfortably in the small tub.

I push the door open.

The room is dark.

Usually, when he's sleeping, he makes a wheezing noise. But tonight the bathroom is silent, eerie.

"Marcus?"

I sweep my hand over the wall, searching for the light switch.

The word *dead* scrolls across my mind. As fast as I erase it, it returns.

Dead. Dead. **DEAD**.

I imagine him lying face down, drowned in the bathtub, my plans for the holidays destroyed.

Where is that damned light switch?

My fingers scurry across the wall, frantic as Freddy Krueger's claw. I'm caught in a nightmare. I find the switch and flick it on. Light spills onto the spick-and-span floor, the spotless walls. The tub—immaculate and empty.

I stare at the white porcelain.

No trace of blood.

No trace of Marcus.

How did he escape?

A white bath towel hangs, neatly folded, on the rack. No stains. Not even a wrinkle.

How did he get out of here?

The room was locked and has no window.

HE HAD HELP.

A secret lover.

Maybe his receptionist?

I pace my apartment, trying to think, but my brain isn't functioning. My thoughts are jumbled, disconnected. My system is going down.

Time for a reality check.

I open the refrigerator, search for the Chia jar. I push aside a bottle of balsamic vinegar, remove a carton of almond milk, and find the jar behind the ketchup. It's filled with Chia seeds. No penises. The jar drops from my hands and seeds scatter across the floor. I'm trembling, feel sick to my stomach.

Who did this?

The super has a key. Maybe she let herself in, stole my penises, absconded with Marcus, who knows what else?

KRISTA pops into my head.

She knows I've been seeing Marcus. She's the only one I told. Obviously she's got a *thing* for him and she's jealous. That's why she's been stalking me, milking me for information.

I pull out my cell phone. Scroll through my contacts. Hit her number.

It rings twice, then she picks up.

"Hi, Sadie."

"Hello, bitch."

"Sadie?"

"Is he there?"

"Who is this?"

"What have you done with him?"

"Who?"

"Marcus."

"Sadie, what are you talking about?"

"Give him back."

I yell into the phone cursing Krista, even after she's clicked off. Her dumb act doesn't fool me. Suddenly it all makes sense—the constant texts, the invitations, the way she's manipulated me.

I run down the hall to the spare room, unlock the freezer, throw open the lid.

My Tupperware and butcher paper packages have vanished. *Lean Cuisines* fill every bin. I don't eat frozen meals. They're full of salt and preservatives.

I've been burglarized!

Or is it burgled?

I want to scream.

I grab my phone, ready to dial 911, prepared to summon Gorski and Redbear. But what will I report? Krista stole my boyfriend, removed him from the bathtub. *No officers, he couldn't take off on his own, because I hacked his legs off with a chainsaw.* On top of that, I'm missing several penises, the rump of a young man, and a thigh I planned to eat for Christmas.

Who will believe me?

My phone vibrates. I glance at the screen, expecting to see Krista's name, but it's my father.

"What? I just got home from work. It's late."

I can barely understand him.

"If you don't like the thong, return it. They give you a shipping label."

While he rambles on about *Victoria's Secret,* I run a bubble bath.

"Why won't they take it back?"

I pass my hand under the faucet, testing the water's temperature.

"You wore it? For an entire week?"

I pull a fresh towel out of the linen closet.

"No. Don't send me your used underpants for Christmas. Why don't you try shopping at a men's store?"

I brew a cup of Kava tea and wash down a few Xanax while my father rants about the lack of customer service, the US Postal Service, the poor selection of men's underwear.

I head back to the bathroom.

Stare into the mirror.

"I've gotta go, Daddy."

I study my reflection, stunned to see a gold Saint Christopher medallion hanging from my neck.

Having rid myself of my father, I do the sensible thing: slide into the bubble bath and buff the muffin with a carrot (organic).

Recipe:
Fried Brains à la Sadie

Many people are afraid of brains, but I don't shy away from them. Generally, you'll want to serve one brain per person, depending on the size, of course. Calf brains are traditional. Personally, I find the donor's level of intelligence determines the brain's flavor, and calves are not particularly smart. Administering an IQ test may be difficult, so you'll have to use your judgment when selecting a brain to suit your taste.

Sadie's Fried Brains

Ingredients:
   1 brain per person
   1 quart cold water
   1 tablespoon vinegar
   Salt and pepper
   All purpose flour
   2 eggs
   ½ cup milk
   1 cup panko breadcrumbs
   5 cloves garlic, minced

½ cup parsley, chopped
2 anchovies, minced
1 teaspoon capers, chopped
½ lemon
1 stick unsalted butter

Preparation:

Soak the brains in a quart of cold water with tablespoon of vinegar for about three hours. Using your fingernails, pick the blood vessels and film off the brains. Soak brains in lukewarm water to remove any traces of blood. To firm them up again, blanch in water with a splash of vinegar. Bring a 2-quart pot of water to simmer, add several cloves of garlic, bay leaf, sprigs of parsley and other fresh herbs, simmer 15 minutes. Gently lower brains into water, for about 6 minutes. Do not boil. Remove to a rack to drain. Season with salt and pepper. When the brains have cooled, if you prefer bite-sized pieces, pull the lobes apart. Skip this step if you prefer them whole.

Prepare 3 bowls: flour, egg whisked with milk, bread-crumbs. Dip brains into each bowl.

Meanwhile melt ½ stick butter in a skillet on medium-high heat. When the butter is frothy, add the brains and sauté until golden and crisp, basting constantly.

Remove to paper towels and keep warm.

In another skillet, melt the other ½ stick of butter. Add minced garlic, parsley, anchovy. Sauté quickly and remove from heat. Add capers and squeeze lemon juice to taste.

Serve brains with the sauce poured over them.

I like to serve this dish with a side of glazed carrots sprinkled with parsley.

STORM

A CRACK OF THUNDER WAKES ME.
I spit out a mouthful of water.

The room is dark. The bath is cold. I might have drowned.

Shivering, I stand, reach blindly for a towel.

Between claps of thunder, I hear pounding—someone's at the front door, demanding entry.

Wrapping myself in the towel, I search for the light switch. Flick it, but nothing happens. The electricity must be out.

I let myself into the hall.

A lightning flash illuminates my living room, and then it's dark.

The pounding on the door gets louder, more insistent.

"Coming!"

Who the hell would visit now, in the middle of a storm?

I walk past the kitchen, feel my way along the couch, trip over a soggy sneaker.

By the time I reach the door, the pounding overrides the thunder.

Peering through the peephole, I can't see a damned thing.

Then I get this creepy feeling.

"Marcus, is that you?"

And then a flashlight blinds me.

"Officers Gorski and Redbear. Open up, Mrs. Bardo."

My fingers freeze on the lock.

"Let us in. Your friend, Krista, called us."

It's too late to pretend that I'm not here.

Too late to claim that I haven't killed Marcus.

Too late to pretend that I haven't disposed of his body—or what remained of it.

I tell myself that everything will be okay. I've scrubbed the place down, cleaned it so thoroughly that I thoroughly fooled myself. They won't find any evidence.

Or will they?

I've been watching *Catching Killers,* the Smithsonian's show about forensics, and these days, one dead cell can provide enough DNA to put me away for life. And Colorado has the death penalty. If I'm going to die, I may as well go out in blaze of gory.

"Open up, or we'll have to force the lock."

Backing away from the door, I let my towel fall to the floor. I'll go out like I came in, naked and alone.

When the pounding starts again, I hear the crack of wood. The cops must have a battering ram. The door strains at its hinges, but I don't stick around to see how long it will hold up.

I run toward the hallway, stumbling over the sneakers. Make it to my bedroom and grope along the wall, until I reach the closet. With trembling hands I manage to part the doors, kick shoes out of my way, searching for the chainsaw. The teeth bite my hand, but I ignore the pain and clutch the handle. Of course, the saw is cold, but it's got fuel. Even in the dark, I find the *on* switch easily, activate the choke, and pull the starter rope. It sputters. Dies.

Out front, I hear what sounds like an explosion.

The cops have made it in.

"Mrs. Bardo?"

I pull the starter rope again, and this time it fires.

Flashlights dance along the hall, then poke their beams into my room, strobe on my naked body.

I rev the chainsaw, turn toward the cops.

"Put that down, Mrs. Bardo. What are you doing?"

"I need firewood."

"Put the chainsaw down, and nothing will happen."

I recognize Gorski's voice, charge toward it, the chainsaw extended.

I'm expecting to hit bodies, expecting to carve through flesh, as easy as carving a Thanksgiving turkey.

But I meet no resistance.

I plunge through the hallway, as the chainsaw gnashes its teeth into the wall. The resulting friction slows me down, throws me off balance.

I hear Gorski yelling, Redbear calling for backup, as I spin through the bathroom's doorway, like a whirling dervish gone berserk—propelled by the weight and power of the chainsaw.

Crashing into the tub, I tumble in, and the chainsaw follows.

"OOOOOOOOWWWWWWWW!!!!!!"

UNDER WARRANTY

C *HOP, CHOP, CHOP.*
Shuck, shuck, shuck.

Wrap, wrap, wrap.

I'm trying not to think.

Thinking slows me down.

Just following the programming.

If I don't think, I can process five cases of corn per hour. That's 240 ears, if there's no mold or worms, forty-eight 5-packs or eighty 3-packs. The supermarket charges $2.99 per 5-pack, so that's a total of $1,495.00; $1.99 per 3-pack equals $1592.00. By my calculations, better profit than they'd get out of a robot—

Thinking, thinking, thinking.

3-packs = greater profit.

STOP!

Thinking is a habit that I'm trying to break. An addiction.

Anyway, I no longer work at the supermarket.

Chop, chop, chop.

Shuck, shuck, shuck.

Wrap, wrap, wrap.

This is the job they've given me, while I wait for my trial.

Krista's husband is my lawyer. For my defense, he's claiming mental incompetence—that's fancy for crazy.

But, between you and me, I'm plenty competent. They're even making me new legs, and I'm holding out for the best (thanks to good insurance): prosthetic calves using carbon nanotubes and neural net technology. My legs will be lighter than titanium and stronger than steel, making me a real Bionic Woman.

Chop, chop, chop.

Really, there's no chopping—I'm not allowed to work with knives.

But they let me shuck.

I'm reading this book, *Chop Wood, Carry Water: A Guide to Finding Spiritual Fulfillment*, about Zen meditation. There's a Zen proverb: "Before Enlightenment chop wood, carry water. After Enlightenment chop wood, carry water."

I view shucking corn as meditation.

Kill.

I don't try to change my thoughts; I watch them.

Kill, kill, kill.

Like clouds passing through a clear blue sky.

Kill, kill, kill, kill, kill, kill, kill, kill.

A Colorado autumn sky.

Corn season is almost over.

The End

Sadie's Food for Thought
Book Club Discussion Questions

1. Is there anyone in your life that you'd like to see dead? If so, why? Are there any similarities between that person and Justus? What would be your preferred method of death? Would you consider murder? How would you dispose of the body? Are you seeing a psychiatrist?

2. Have you ever worked with a robot? Do you feel threatened by robots? If so, why? If not, what do you like about robots? Would you date a robot? Consider marriage? Does the idea of downloading your brain into a robot turn you on?

3. Talk about Sadie's various methods of murder. Which one most appeals to you? Which would you avoid? Would you like Sadie to be your neighbor? Have you ever had a neighbor like Sadie? Are you a neighbor like Sadie?

4. Do you plan to try any of Sadie's recipes? Would you follow the directions or make modifications? What modifications will you make? Have you considered a potluck for the next book club meeting?

5. Has reading the book affected how you feel about shopping at supermarkets? Do you bring your own bags? Insist on using paper? Prefer plastic? How do you feel about salmonella? E coli? Falling into a trash compactor?

6. Talk about plot. How would your plotting of murder differ from Sadie's? What mistakes did she make? How might she improve her methods? Do you think she's sex crazed or are her appetites fairly normal? And what's with eating her psychiatrist—is that symbolic or is she saving on groceries?

7. Compare this book to others you have read. Can you imagine Sadie in a book by Jane Austen? How do you think Mr. Darcy would react to Sadie? And how do you think Sadie would respond to Mr. Darcy? If Mr. Darcy came to dinner, what would Sadie serve?

8. Finally, did this book make you think? Did you learn anything? Do you feel sorry for Sadie? Would you like to see more of her? Do you want to meet Sadie's dad? If so, please send your phone number and Sadie will have him call you.

ACKNOWLEDGEMENTS

W RITING A BOOK INVOLVES A lot of people. I would like to thank my friend and mentor, author Blake Crouch, who encouraged me to lengthen a short story into a novel and offered welcome advice. Other early readers who encouraged me include authors Elizabeth Cratty and Gail Harris. Poet, Haz Saïd, offered me some great (especially dark) ideas, and I appreciate his continual encouragement. Feedback from my beta readers was priceless: Blake Crouch, Terry Junttonen, Haz Saïd, Terry McClaren, Deborah Warner, and Tory Hartmann (no relation to the character in the book—except they both have red hair and like designer clothes).

Jeroen ten Berge designed yet another amaaazing cover. My copy editor, Diana Cox, caught all my misplaced dashes. And Terry Roy has done a brilliant job of formatting.

Thank you!

Other Books

Zané Sachs is currently working on *Jayne Just Watches,* a novel of psychological horror and suspense. She expects to release the book at the end of 2014.

Contact Zané Sachs

ZaneSachs@gmail.com

http://zanesachs.com/

Blog: *Zané Sachs*-**Going Down** (http://zanesachs.com/)

Zané Sachs on Facebook (https://www.facebook.com/ZaneSachs)

@Zané Sachs on Twitter (https://twitter.com/ZaneSachs)

Zané Sachs at Google+

Made in the USA
Middletown, DE
18 August 2017